A Perfect Danger

PHILLIPA NEFRI CLARK

A Perfect Danger

PHILLIPA NEFRI CLARK

Prologue

"It has to be here."

In the dark office on the twenty-seventh floor, Nellie Sinclair rifled through a drawer in her boss's desk. Floor to ceiling windows overlooked Sydney Harbour Bridge, a breathtaking view night or day. Just not at this moment.

The landline on his desk rang, and she jumped, dropping the handful of papers she'd just lifted. They slid onto the floor, fanning out, no longer in order. She knelt and collected them, sorting, ignoring the endless ringing. Nobody was here to answer. It was two in the morning. Even workaholic Andre Canning was tucked up in a bed somewhere. Someone's bed. So, whoever was trying to reach him was out of luck.

Papers fixed, she checked the back of the drawer using a pencil torch, muttering beneath her breath when there was nothing more than some loose business cards and a pen. But as she shoved the papers in, they caught on something on the underside of the drawer above. She peeled the tape away and finally held the object in her palm.

Who would believe something so small held such power? Nellie let out a long, slow breath.

"This isn't the time for this discussion." A male voice was outside the office door.

Nellie had never moved so fast in her life. What the heck was Andre doing here? She had the drawer closed and was across the room in seconds. Waiting in the shadows at the door his secretary used, she listened.

"There's never a time, is there?"

She didn't recognise the voice of the other speaker. Male. American. Different from Andre's North Shore's educated nuances.

"Alright then. While I wholeheartedly agree that Carlo Bianchi is on borrowed time, my way is the right one. What you recorded that night is everything I need to—"

"Disagree, boss. He'll have you behind bars in hours if you use it as leverage."

Wrapping her fingers more tightly around the small object she'd stolen, Nellie knew she'd done the right thing.

"Which is why I am the boss. You don't know him the way I do."

A key rattled in the lock of the main door. Thank goodness Andre used old-fashioned locks as extra security instead of relying on key cards and that she'd locked it from the inside. Getting caught was not an option.

Nellie felt behind herself for the knob and carefully turned it until the door gave.

"Then why haven't you confronted him?"

"Because you and I are not the only ones to have seen the footage."

"The girl? Just get rid of her, Andre. Why risk the liability?"

"Because I like her, Spence. Always have. She's cute, in

that serious, brainy-but-beautiful way. Just once, I'd like to run my fingers through those long, blonde waves."

Touching her hair—currently tied back in a ponytail—a tide of nausea rose in Nellie's stomach. How could he...ergh. They'd worked together for years, gone away to conferences, attended functions. Had he really thought...

Ergh!

She slipped through the doorway, closing the door bit by bit. Had she properly shut the drawer? Nellie peered through the remaining crack. All the drawers were closed.

Her heart almost stopped.

Beneath the desk, a stray sheet of paper taunted her. She'd missed it when retrieving the papers she'd dropped. Was there time to sprint over and grab it?

The main office door opened, but Andre was still talking to the other man, his back to Nellie. It was too far to risk. All it would take was him turning, and she'd be caught.

"Mate, keep your gross fantasies to yourself and tell me why I'm even here if not to do your dirty work."

"Patience." Andre stepped inside, reaching for the light switch. Nellie had the door closed before it came on and held her breath, listening in case he'd picked up the slight movement, but their voices continued as before, just muffled.

Using the darkness to her advantage, Nellie slipped through the secretary's office, which shared the wall with Andre's one but had no door or front wall. She peered around the corner. The other man leaned against Andre's doorframe, talking to him. He was almost bald, wiry, and a bit under six feet. There was no chance of getting past unless he went right in thanks to the open floor plan apart from Andre's lockable space. The lifts and stairs were on the far side of the floor.

I can't be seen. I can't lose this now.

She pocketed the object. If she was caught with it, there'd be a high price to pay. Stealing from anyone was bad. But stealing from Andre Canning was to bring his wrath and connections after her. Though there was no alternative Nellie hadn't already considered and discarded.

"What's this?"

"Duh...a piece of paper, Andre. Something found in offices the world over."

"Not mine. Not carelessly left on the floor. Not ever." Andre's tone was sharp and annoyed.

His friend stepped into the office and Nellie took off, running crouched down to use the dividers between desks as cover. Never had the distance from his office to the stairwell seemed so vast, but she made it to the lifts and went straight past. There was no way the men wouldn't hear the ding as the lift arrived. She flew around another corner to the fire door and took a few precious seconds to open it as quietly as she could. The heavy door was harder to close, taking so long for the hydraulic arm to work it back into its place and despite keeping the handle turned, there was a noticeable click when it shut.

Nellie raced down the stairs. Three flights and then a tell-tale thud came from above as the fire door was breached.

She flattened against the wall, the cold from the concrete chilling her spine. Her heart raced at a million miles an hour and her breath came in short, sharp bursts, which she fought to control.

"Who's there? Come back. We'll negotiate." Andre's voice echoed down the space.

Right. With a bullet?

The door closed, and she took off again as footsteps thumped.

There was no chance she could make it down another twenty-something floors. One of them was chasing her. The other would take the lift and wait for her at the bottom.

At the eighteenth floor, her fingers hovered over the panel beside the fire door.

"Five-seven-two-three...no...five-seven-three-two-nine-six-six."

Yes!

It turned to green and the door unlocked. She didn't wait for it to close behind her. Her pursuer was several flights of stairs behind and the fire door would close well before he realised where she'd gone. He'd keep going and meet with Andre—for she was certain her boss wouldn't run down stairs—at the bottom. Then they had a mammoth job ahead.

Nellie knew every inch of the building, all thirty floors and this one belonged to a different company, one Andre had nothing to do with. She was safe here for a short time thanks to knowing the access code of her best friend, Cory. Even if those men worked out she was in here, all she had to do was wait until business hours and get Cory to help her exit. In daylight, and with thousands of workers, she'd have her best chance.

She dropped onto the floor on her hands and knees. Exhausted not just from the escape but the mental and emotional drain from the past few days. The footage Andre had so proudly shown her had turned her carefully controlled world upside-down.

Thump. Thump. Thump.

Whoever was kicking that fire door wasn't happy.

"What have I got myself into?"

Chapter One

Three months later.

This was *nothing* like the pictures from the real estate agent.

Nellie came to a halt at the bottom of the steps of the farmhouse she'd bought, dropping her suitcase onto the ground in shock.

The verandah was a far cry from the painted white weatherboards, love seat, and planter boxes she'd fallen in love with from the images the real estate agent had sent. Instead of wide, freshly stained steps with flower pots over-flowing with daisies on either side, cracked and—frankly—dangerous looking planks of timber were decidedly lacking in floral arrangements.

Her torch darted from broken railings to holes in the timber decking to a smashed window. Spider webs draped the corner above the door. Was this even the right place?

She'd had no choice but to buy the property remotely. Since that fateful night in Sydney, she'd had to keep moving, keep her head down. The decision to bury herself somewhere nobody would think of looking was made out of desperation. Renting wouldn't work because she'd need references and a history and put herself at risk of exposure. But buying a furnished farmhouse in the middle of nowhere was perfect.

Until it wasn't.

Thunder boomed, and the wind picked up. The storm had followed her for hours, always in the car's rear vision mirror on the drive from Newcastle, where she'd stayed with one of Cory's cousins for the past month. Before then, it was Sydney's northern beaches, where Cory had kept her safe while she sorted out her future. Well, it had caught up with her now and from the lightning crackling across the sky, things were about to turn nasty.

Heart thudding, Nellie picked up the suitcase and climbed the half-dozen steps which creaked under her weight.

She paused, key in hand, unsure of herself. What if this wasn't the house she'd bought? What if she'd missed a turn on the difficult, dark road? But she had to find out.

The key turned the lock, and the door opened with an ominous creak.

At least nobody will look for me here! I wouldn't.

She found a light switch. She'd arranged for the power to be on. It was the one reason she'd kept driving, knowing she'd soon be in her new home with light and warmth and somewhere to sleep without fear. But the light didn't turn on. She flipped the switch a few times, but still the light didn't turn on. The house shook as thunder cracked overhead and rain suddenly hammered onto the metal roof.

She couldn't drive back to Bindarra Creek, which was

the closest town in this weather, and where would she even find an open motel at this hour? Nellie mentally kicked herself for not thinking this through.

She should have taken her time getting here.

Stayed somewhere else overnight.

Had the house inspected instead of buying it sight unseen.

Told the police everything...

Closing the front door, she put the suitcase down and shone the torch around. She was in a wide and long hallway with rooms going off either side and an archway at the far end. The place was huge. Closest was a living room with a broken sofa and a cobweb-covered chandelier. The rug was threadbare beneath her tired feet, but there were timber floorboards. Nice ones.

Something landed on her head and she squealed, her hand flicking through her now not-quite shoulder-length hair. No spiders. Her fingers were wet. Nellie raised the torch to the ceiling. Heavy drops of water formed on the plaster, then fell.

Halfway between a laugh and a sob, she whispered, "Welcome to your new life, Annalise."

The rest of the house was just as bad, possibly made worse by the lack of lighting and booming thunder.

At least it was the size they said it would be. Nellie had to give the agent credit for that, if nothing else. The place was huge. Five bedrooms. Two bathrooms—thank goodness the facilities worked—and a spacious laundry with a door leading outside. She took one look at the kitchen and left. What appeared to be someone's dinner from years ago was on an old table in the middle. Tomorrow, with daylight, she'd revisit it.

With gloves and a garbage bag and probably a mask.

She went back through the front door to gaze at the night. Standing on the verandah, she breathed deeply of air made fresh by rain. It was different here from Sydney. Despite the storm or maybe because of it, there was a sense of isolation...but not in a scary way. Not how her life had been for weeks on end since stealing from Andre. No, here was safe. Secluded and protected from unwanted eyes by bushland and distance.

If only she could relax. Even just for a while. Stop looking over her shoulder for a shadow on her tail. With a last glance back at the driveway and her poor car being belted by rain, Nellie closed and locked the front door.

The room she figured to be a living room had some furniture, but the only usable piece was one oversized armchair with no obvious holes, deterioration, or mould. That would do as her bed.

I've slept in worse places.

But try as she might, Nellie's determination to see the best of the situation was crumbling. This might have been the biggest mistake of her life—well, the second biggest. One led to the other. She refused to regret the theft. The stakes were too high for second-guessing her decision to take from him the one thing he valued more than life— other people's lives, anyway. It should have been in a safe or a security deposit box, but the man had serious issues about trusting devices of any kind, so she'd been pretty confident she'd find it in his office.

Opening her suitcase, she pulled out a blanket and

thanked her past self for thinking about adding it. There was a small esky with enough for her trip and she took an apple and a bottle of water, then settled on the armchair, curling up to watch the lightning display through windows which might once have been beautiful. Tomorrow would take care of itself. Tonight, she needed sleep.

Hunger roused Nellie from dreams of shadowy pursuers and spiders falling on her head.

The rain had stopped and a beam of sunlight jitterbugged with dust motes. She stretched and stood, moaning when her muscles complained from too long a drive and sleeping in an armchair.

What if I can't make this place habitable?

She pushed the panic down. One step at a time.

Nellie considered herself to be a careful person. One who thought things through, made plans, evaluated risk. Her entire adult life was a testament to this. A solid career as a graphic designer in a prestigious company. Hard working. Sensible about money. And no jumping out of airplanes or into relationships. It worked for her.

Until the day she overheard a startling conversation and was shown an even more concerning video taken on a phone.

Her head dropped. Never had she taken a risk so dangerous. But there'd been no choice.

I did the right thing and I'll live with the consequences.

Working out if this house was fixable was the first of them.

Half an hour later, she'd unpacked her car, putting

boxes, more suitcases, and a few creature comforts into the living room. Going in and out of the house helped with the familiarity and she discovered which parts of which step to stand on. She moved the car under a carport she'd not noticed last night. It was along the side of the house toward the back. And as she returned to the front of the house, she came to an abrupt halt as a kangaroo bounded by.

Joy bubbled up and suddenly she was smiling. A lifetime of living in the city had never given her such delight as this one simple moment in the country.

Instead of going back inside, she wandered down the sloping driveway. Last night she'd been careful to keep on the narrow dirt track, afraid of the car getting stuck in mud —even though it was an SUV. This morning, as sunlight warmed the ground, a fine steam lifted in wisps, forming ghosts which dissipated as they rose. Birdsong filled the air and cockatoos screeched to one another from the tops of gum trees scattered around the property.

It was perhaps a hundred metres to the entry and once Nellie reached it, she stopped in awe at the bushland surrounding her. A dirt road was the only sign of civilisation as far as she could see. From the research she'd done before buying the house, there were no neighbours for some distance—certainly none along this dead-end road. It was the first thing which had made her shortlist the place. There was a tiny little town, well, a hamlet really with maybe half a dozen shops, but most of the population seemed to live on the far side of the main road leading to Armidale.

The land was about ten acres in size. The agent called it a bushland retreat—more like an overgrown bush block —but she had no idea where the boundaries were yet and couldn't see fencing on either side thanks to dense bushes. Or could they be the boundary? There was no front fence.

The sound of a vehicle approached, and she froze, her heart pounding. Surely, he hadn't found her? The growl of the motor drew closer, galvanising her into action. As the bonnet of a large 4WD appeared along the road, she dived behind a tree.

It sounded as though it slowed.

Is it turning in?

For a long moment, the vehicle idled outside the driveway and then, just as Nellie thought she'd need to make a run for it—though to where she didn't know—it moved on. She peered around the trunk as it moved past and, once she was certain she couldn't be seen, Nellie ran down to the side of the road.

The 4WD was going into another driveway a couple of hundred metres away, right on a dead end. It pulled up and someone climbed out, too far for her to see much detail apart from a brief impression of a tall and well-built man about her age who went to open a farm gate. When he returned, he paused near the bonnet, staring across the distance at her. There was nothing familiar about him. Not Andre. Nor the other man from that night—he'd been shorter and thin. But she wasn't taking any chances and hurried back to the safety of her own driveway and kept going.

On the way up, she tried to see through the trees along the side of the property where the 4WD had gone. Through a tiny gap, she was certain she spotted another house. Short of leaving the driveway to get a better look, that fleeting impression had to do for now.

As she reached the top of her steps, she cast a look in the direction of her neighbour. This was a complication she'd not expected. Her research hadn't shown a neighbouring house down the dead-end road. Clearly, her research was a failure. With a bit of luck, he'd keep to himself and leave her alone to deal with starting over from scratch.

Chapter Two

As her first day in the house progressed, Nellie's mood had swung back and forth between despair and a subdued hope.

The more she inspected her new home, the more she wanted to have a short, sharp conversation with the real estate agent. There was probably a law against misleading a buyer so badly, but her back was against the wall and she was too exhausted to run any longer.

A phone call to the local electricity company at least reassured her she'd have power tomorrow, but for now, she faced another night in the dark. She'd discarded the idea of moving to a motel because if she'd been followed, it would be an obvious place to look.

Unpacking the car reminded her how woefully unprepared she was for a new life.

Two suitcases of clothing, shoes, and other personal items were the bare minimum to get her through the next few weeks. Thank goodness for summer because once the weather turned cold, she'd need to buy appropriate clothes. She had enough bedding for now, a pillow, sheets, a blanket, and a lightweight sleeping bag. If all else failed, she'd sleep on the floor until she found some decent furniture.

One thing she was thankful for was the foresight to bring a fully charged, long-life power bank. It would keep her phone and laptop going until the power came on. And she was getting some coverage, intermittent, but better than nothing.

After the scare of discovering a neighbour, she'd locked herself in the house for a while, checking through the windows and pacing up and down the long hallway. What if the man in the 4WD wasn't a neighbour at all? What if he worked for Andre and somehow had uncovered her new life? This constant feeling of having to look over her shoulder was understandable but had to stop or she'd go crazy with worry. She wanted to live here. Wanted to build a new life for herself and forget the toxic world she'd left behind.

"And it starts now, Nellie."

Before she could change her mind, she picked up her handbag, locked the front door on her way out, and went to her car. Food, water—because what came out of the pipes was disgusting—and cleaning products were high on her list of shopping items and hopefully she wouldn't need to go too far to shop. She carefully turned out of her driveway, checking nobody was coming from the direction of the other house. Was that the only other one around here, or had she simply not seen other driveways in the storm last night?

The narrow dirt road was the only way in and out, at least according to her phone's map. It wound through heavy bushland and she slowed after a flock of galahs almost flew into her. Apart from a few potholes, the surface wasn't terrible to drive on, but passing an oncoming vehicle would require moving onto the shoulder...in the few places there was one. She was thankful to have an SUV, even if it was a few years old. Being a little higher than her last car, a sporty number she regretted selling, had its advantages and the benefits of off-road handling would help on this terrain. After a few minutes, she reached Mt. Ingalls Road and turned left.

Just over a bridge was Glenmeer central. If one was as kind as to call it that. The handful of shops didn't boast a supermarket, so she kept going. Another day, she'd stop and wander to see what was on offer, but her first impression didn't excite her.

This isn't Sydney. Get used to it.

She accelerated as she reached the open road, pushing down a sudden urge to cry.

Would she ever return to the world she knew? For almost her entire adult life, she'd owned an apartment in Manly and she'd spent every waking moment on the beach when she wasn't working. Everyone knew her heart belonged to the sea, which was a deciding factor in finding a new home as opposite as possible. She and Andre had spent many hours on beaches around the world in their downtime from business events and he used to call her a 'beach baby' and then make a stupid attempt at singing the Beach Boys' song.

"I won't miss your singing. Or you."

Talking aloud helped manage her emotions.

"But I miss my job. And my beautiful home and friends."

The last bit was a bit of a stretch. Not many friends, thanks to the long hours she poured into her job. And Andre's insistence she be as available for clients at the drop of a hat.

"How are you managing without me?"

She grinned at that. He had his secretary, but nobody apart from Andre understood the design needs of his company the way Nellie did. It was his fault she'd left. After her discovery, there was no way she'd have stayed working for him.

"And after I stole your precious data, there's no way I'd have stayed alive for long."

The countryside was beautiful and beneath a clear sky, she couldn't stay down for long. Her life had changed— perhaps forever—but her spirit and ethics were the same. Whatever adventures lay ahead were exactly that, adventures.

The first adventure was navigating around Bindarra Creek township. By no means a large town, it nevertheless had character and a certain street appeal. Nellie found a supermarket and parked in its carpark, electing to find something for a late lunch before shopping. Breakfast had been the last of her stock of apples and she'd not realised how hungry she was until she climbed out of the car. A kind woman sent her in the direction of the Cypress Café, where she managed to buy a sausage roll and a bottle of ginger beer. She found a bench on the way back and sat, devouring the delicious bakery food for minutes. The afternoon was warm and humid, not as bad as Sydney's relentless summer mugginess, but enough to remind her she needed to buy some new hats. Another day.

The supermarket was cool and well stocked, and she picked up more than planned. There were premade salads which were perfect given she had no refrigeration. Add some cheese and a bread roll and that was dinner sorted. More rolls for breakfast and lunch tomorrow with a couple of small tins of baked beans and tuna. Some fruit and bottled water, and she was set for food. After adding rubbish bags, disposable gloves, scourers, cleaning cloths and a range of cleaning products, she went through the checkout, paying in cash and politely declining to join the loyalty program. Maybe the time would come when she would give out her personal details to strangers.

She stowed her groceries and drove out, forgetting which way was home and heading back past the cafe. Rather than try to turn back, she kept going around the streets, which were several blocks of shops and businesses. A hardware store encouraged her to pull over.

For a few minutes, Nellie didn't move. She watched cars and people, all innocent passers-by who were going about their day-to-day business, unaware they had a thief among them. How would these nice folks of Bindarra Creek react if they knew she was hiding here? Relocating by necessity. Would they demand she leave? Call the authorities?

Nellie shivered and ran a hand across her eyes.

"Stop panicking. Come on, stop it."

She grabbed her handbag, yanked the keys from the ignition, and climbed out. After locking the car...and checking twice it was locked, she hurried into the hardware shop. Basket in hand, she stood in the middle of an aisle.

"Need a hand, love?" A white-haired man with a logo on his shirt offered a kindly smile. "I tend to get lost in the beauty of hardware myself."

His friendly face helped her relax. This was a tiny town in the middle of nowhere. Andre had no idea she was here. And her new house was in desperate need of repair.

"Actually, I could use some advice."

By early evening, Nellie had made a detailed list of issues she needed to address. She'd also created another list of what was useable in the house. It was a short list and would depend upon what happened once the electricity was on.

There was a refrigerator, which surprised her with a spotless interior. It was at least ten years old, but looked in good shape. If it worked, that was a bonus. The tap over the sink worked, but the water was disgusting and even after she'd let it run for a few minutes, hadn't cleared of silt. She'd need someone to look at the water tank she could see through the grimy window, and perhaps check the pipes.

She donned gloves and opened a large garbage bag. Last night, under torchlight, she'd assumed the paper bags, plastic takeaway containers, and fast-food wrappers scattered over the kitchen table were from ages ago. Perhaps last meals as the occupants were leaving.

"Then what is this?" Between her thumb and one finger, Nellie lifted the corner of white paper...like from a fish and chips shop. Beneath it were a handful of soggy chips that couldn't have been more than a few days old. She dropped the corner as if it was poison and stepped back, heart thumping. Who'd been in her house?

Ignoring the urge to check every room, she went to the back door. It was the only door she hadn't opened and when she turned the knob, it swung open with a creak. There was no lock, just holes in the door where one must have been, once.

Anyone could have walked in here while she was sleeping.

Andre or his friend might be here somewhere, hiding outside, waiting for dark.

That man next door...was this a message that she was vulnerable and to watch out?

Nellie ran from the kitchen, yelping as she banged her shoulder against a door frame. In the living room, she began to throw unpacked items into a box. She had to leave. Did she even have time to pack? The room was spinning, and she had to drop into the armchair to catch her breath. Between exhaustion and hunger and worry, she was going to make herself ill. Running wasn't the solution. She willed her breathing to slow and her panic to subside.

Maybe she had a short-term fix. She slowly stood. No more spinning. Thanking past Nellie for stopping at the hardware shop, Nellie dug through the bags of purchases. Her fingers were shaking too much, and she upturned the contents onto the chair. Packets of nails in several sizes. A screwdriver and screws. Adhesive patches to manage some of the leaks. And locks with chains. Three of them.

"Thank goodness," she muttered. From the other bag, she took a hammer and a pair of scissors and then hurried back to the kitchen. When her attempt to rip open the packaging around the lock failed, she cut it off in big slices, small screws tipped out onto the floor. For a moment she stared at the little pieces of metal rolling around at her feet, her hands clenching and unclenching as she fought for control. Rather than cry, she closed her eyes and went to her happy place.

The sand squelches between my toes. Pleasantly warm. Breathing in the tang of the sea, I taste salt on my lips. And as the sand becomes firmer beneath my feet, cool water whooshes over my skin. The wave recedes. Then returns. Recedes. Returns.

Opening her eyes, she put her hand on her heart. It

seemed to beat normally, not that she was medically trained, but the pounding was gone. She had to accept it would take a while to feel safe. "More meditation. Less reactivity." She touched the pendant she now always wore. "And this is why."

One by one she picked up the screws, worked out how the lock attached to the wall and door, and set about her new job. Doing was better than thinking. She finished and repeated the process in the laundry and then the front door. Every action was one step closer to having a secure place to hide. To live.

That done, she worked on sleeping arrangements. By now it was dark outside and she turned on two battery operated lanterns, leaving one in the kitchen and carrying the other into the bedrooms. There was a dismantled double bed frame in one. And leaning against the wall in another bedroom was a mattress which would fit the frame. It was brand new, still in heavy plastic. Such an odd find, but one she wasn't about to question. She'd already decided the front bedroom, with a lovely view, was in the best state of repair. At least in here were floorboards rather than stinky old carpet found in a few of the other rooms. She'd bought a mop and bucket from the hardware store and gave the floorboards the best clean she could, using cold water, then carried the bed pieces to the room.

As a graphic designer, Nellie knew how to create elements and turn them into a cohesive whole. So surely a bed was simple? One headpiece, one endpiece, and a middle. After leaning the bed head against a wall, she lined up the base and let out a soft 'yes!' when the pieces slipped into place. The joy was short lived as the downward facing prongs on the far end of the base refused to go into the foot of the bed.

Thank goodness for the hammer. A few decent whacks and the bed was done. She dragged the mattress in and cut the plastic off, almost losing her footing on the still-wet floor as she manoeuvred it onto the frame. The addition of sheets and her blanket gave a homely feel...or as close as she was going to get at this point.

She made a quick bathroom stop and found herself staring at the shower.

How wonderful to have a hot shower, glass of wine, and sleep to the sound of the ocean.

None of which was going to happen tonight. One final thing before eating. Check the car was locked. She knew it was, but would worry all night if she didn't check. How on earth had she become so obsessive about rechecking herself? On the way back up the front steps, one of them collapsed, and she grabbed the railing with a loud, "Dammit".

She righted herself and checked the damage. Nothing a new piece of timber wouldn't fix, but as she straightened, something in the distance caught her eye. Something white against the dark bushland, slightly higher where the ground rose toward the next property.

Nellie had never seen a white kangaroo or any other large, white-coloured Australian animal likely to be on her property. Had she imagined it? She turned off the lantern and scanned the area. It was in the direction of her neighbour. Was he watching her?

If he was one of Andre's people, here to recover what she'd stolen, she was in trouble. Lots of places to bury a body out here.

Action, not speculation.

She rushed up the remaining steps and collected a torch.

Back outside, she spent a few minutes casting its light as far as it would go...which wasn't far enough. Another trip to the hardware store was in order, and this time she'd take a long list.

It hadn't been her imagination. But whatever she'd seen wasn't there now, and she wasn't inclined to investigate.

Time to eat, Nellie. Then, time to sleep.

Chapter Three

"I reckon you need your eyes tested. Told you moving right out here with no human company apart from your clients would lead to hallucinations." Blair Maxwell grinned.

Kane—older brother by several years and infinitely more sensible, in his own opinion of course—finished constructing two homemade burgers and then headed for the oven. "Don't you have to go back to Sydney?"

"Sure do. Not for a week, though. So, tell me about this imaginary woman?"

Kane had wondered himself if he'd been seeing things earlier, but there was definitely someone moving in next door. He grabbed an oven mitt and removed a tray of home-made potato wedges. Those went into a bowl, followed by a sprinkle of pink salt. The vegetable patch out the back had yielded a bumper crop of potatoes, which were in paper bags in a dark part of the pantry. Nothing beat the fresh-ness of his own produce, even if he hadn't yet worked out how to grow just enough for himself and to give to his parents when he saw them. Instead, it was always more than expected.

"Dude? Beer?"

"Thanks. I'll take these outside." Kane carried the plates with the burgers through the house, pushing the front screen door open with a hip.

The verandah was his favourite place to eat. He'd got a small table and chairs set up on the corner closest to...well, the new neighbour. If she turned out to be a person who hosted noisy parties, he'd rethink the positioning, but for now, the only sound was his brother clomping on the floor-boards behind him.

"Did you want sauce at all? I bought some. Tomato, mayo, and aioli."

"Yeah."

Blair put the bowl down and three jars of the before-mentioned condiments, all made by their mother. "Be right back."

Peace again. Kane gazed over to the old house next door. He could see part of it from here. In the state it was in why would anyone move in?

"What? Looking for your phantom woman?" Blair just didn't give up. At least he'd brought the beers with him this time. "Are you sure you weren't drinking?"

"Funny. This, kid, is my first for the week."

And it tasted like heaven. Kane's week was one he'd like to forget. Two groups and one individual, booked on different days for the same basic tour. A night out in Akuna National Park, camping beneath the stars and a few hours gentle hiking. The two groups were hard going as none of the guests had a clue about the bush and he'd ended up setting up almost everything as they stood by watching. The individual—a woman—had been out of her depth from the beginning, which irked Kane. It wasn't typical of women who wanted to visit the park but this one went from being overly confident before they set out to needing help with every aspect of what was a tame tour. He'd wondered several times if it was a show. She'd even gone as far as to ask him to carry her over a creek. Which he hadn't done.

"Earth to Kane."

"What's the problem?" Kane helped himself to a wedge and spooned some aioli on before taking a bite. Delicious crisp-on-the-outside and fluffy inside potato paired perfectly with the creamy, garlicky dressing.

"I asked if you were expecting a neighbour. I mean, hasn't that place been empty for years? I heard it was haunted and the previous occupants left in a hurry."

"I think you are weak from hunger. Eat something."

Blair chuckled and picked up his burger.

"To answer the question, no. If anything, I've been half-expecting someone to bulldoze the old house and start over. Do you remember I originally looked at that place first? The land is smaller than I wanted. And the house? Needs a lot of work."

Blair finished his mouthful with a nod. "This one did as well."

"True. But the foundation was good. And you helped a heap with new weatherboard and the decking and stuff."

Putting down his burger, Blair rose his beer and lifted an eyebrow. "Praise? I'll take that."

"Facts. But sure, take it as praise."

Both of them burst into laughter then clinked the necks of the beers together.

As they ate, the sun dipped behind the top of the gum trees, casting long shadows across the stretch of short grass at the front of the house. There was still an hour or so of daylight left and for once, Kane wasn't inclined to put it to good use. He usually worked from dawn to dark, either in or on his business, or around the property. It suited his nature to stay busy and both the business—which was still young—and this acreage, took most of his energy.

"Decent meal, Kane. Fills the spot."

"Thanks. I wonder if she has food." His eyes drifted back to the other house. "Doubt if there's power on so no fridge. No oven. Not like we have a fast-food franchise in Glenmeer."

"Should we take her a picnic?" Blair asked. "Cupcakes, wine, the rest of these wedges..."

"I'm serious." Kane took the last two from the bowl before Blair could. "You know, I thought I saw headlights last night, right in the middle of the storm. But it never occurred to me anyone would be going to the old house. Don't even remember anyone looking around to buy it."

"Except you are away most of the time."

True.

Blair stood and went to the side railing, straining to see the other house. "All looks quiet. Maybe she was doing an inspection rather than moving in."

"Saw her car leave earlier and then return."

"Do you want to check on her?"

And do what? Welcome her to the neighbourhood of two houses with a cup of sugar?

Earlier he'd almost gone past the first driveway but a sudden movement in his peripheral vision made him stop. That old house had sat vacant for as long as he could remember and the last thing he wanted in the middle of a hot summer were squatters or kids who might start a fire. At the top of the long driveway an SUV was just visible parked under the carport.

Deciding it was none of his concern, Kane had headed

home. After opening his gate, he got the oddest sensation he was being watched and looked back down the road. A young woman with white-blonde hair stared at him. It was a fair distance, but he had decent eyesight and got the impression she was poised to run.

Why were you scared?

"So, are we making a picnic?"

"No, we are minding our own business. Why are you home tonight? I thought you'd be spending the evening at your girlfriend's place."

Dropping back into his seat, Blair shook his head. "Miranda and Pop Layton were invited to dinner at Beryl's house...to meet some of her family who are visiting. Miranda hasn't met any of them yet. For that matter, she still barely knows Beryl."

"Must be strange seeing her grandfather with another woman. She's taken it well." Kane missed Nan Layton who'd always welcomed him and Blair at their home in Bindarra Creek. She'd passed away a few years ago, and it was only late last year Pop began seeing Beryl. "But then again," he grinned at Blair. "You're keeping her too busy to have time to worry."

Blair reddened.

It was satisfying, And cute.

"Well...Miranda and I are trying to enjoy each other's company before I go away again." Blair picked up the beer and played with the almost-empty bottle. "We're just lucky to have had this window of time together, with her grooming salon closed until next week. I feel as if we're making up for all the years we didn't know we loved each other."

Blair's voice softened. He gazed in the direction where —many kilometres away in Bindarra Creek—Miranda lived. This new love of theirs was the only possible result for two people who'd been best friends for so long and all joking aside, it made Kane happy.

But a little part of him, deep down, was heavy. Not for his brother but himself. He'd loved and lost and wasn't going down that path again. He had everything he needed in life.

There were no lights on at the old house when Kane took the rubbish out but there was hammering.

He wandered in the direction of the farm fencing at the edge of his property, not bothering with a torch. Tonight, the sky was clear and moonlight cut through the canopy of trees. A marked difference from the weather last night which made him abandon the overnight camping part of the tour, much to the annoyance of the woman who'd suggested they see the night out in the back of his vehicle.

He shuddered. Might be time to look more closely at only accepting overnight tours with multiple guests.

The hammering stopped as he reached the fence. From here, his own house was almost invisible behind scrub but the old place next door was in clear view. This far away, a hundred or so metres, one could be excused for believing it was in good shape. It had a classic wide wrap-around verandah beneath the roofline, weatherboards, and a tin roof. It sat toward the back of the property with a stretch of open ground between it and the start of the National Park. Whoever had originally built the two homes had done so with the weather extremes in mind and they'd been well constructed. But ten or more years abandoned was enough to damage any house.

A light bobbed around through a front window and then came onto the verandah and down the steps. The woman he'd seen earlier was carrying a lantern. So, he was right. No power. She might not have running water either. There was a big tank but goodness knows what condition the contents were like after a decade of stagnation.

He sighed. At this rate he'd have to drop in if only to let her know how long since any maintenance was done.

Well. Maybe she knows. If she can use a hammer, she probably bought it as a fixer-upper.

All that thought did was make him bristle. There'd been talk of developers in the area. Was she the first of many looking to renovate and sell to city folk? He'd chosen his property for its seclusion and wouldn't sit back if anyone wanted to sub-divide or put in a helipad.

"Dammit!"

The voice echoing across was clearly frustrated. And decidedly attractive with a low, husky tone. It also galvanised Kane and he moved up the fence line toward a spot he knew he could easily climb over. If something was wrong, he should help. But even as he pushed down on the wire, the stilling of the lantern made him pause.

Not only did it stop moving, but it was extinguished.

He waited, eyes straining to see if she was okay. That she hadn't fallen or had some other misadventure. There was nothing at all for a few minutes and then, just as he'd decided to go and check, a light shone in his direction. Not enough to pick him up from such a distance but he'd been noticed and rather than be caught watching a stranger, he slipped behind a tree.

This wasn't the way to meet a new neighbour.

Chapter Four

Sleep was a joke.

Although the bed was surprisingly comfortable, Nellie found herself back in the kitchen not long after midnight. She opened her laptop on the now-pristine table and tethered the phone to use its internet.

I would murder for a coffee.

No power. No coffee. And nowhere close to run out and get one.

She sighed dramatically and laughed at herself. What she did have was a huge block of chocolate which somehow found itself in her shopping basket earlier. She snapped a row off as she waited to connect. Her intention was to start the search for some tradespeople to help put this house into a habitable state, but instead, she typed the website address of her old job.

Canning and Hayward Advertising.

She almost exited the second the site loaded. But

curiosity got the better of her and with a click, she was on Andre's profile page.

The same photo she'd approved two years ago stared back. A power image. Andre sat—open legged—on an expensive sofa, leaning forward with his elbows on his legs and hands clasped as he gazed at the camera. There was the slightest of smiles on his lips and his stare was intense. And the photo-manipulated to make those blue eyes of his even bluer and be the centre of attention.

There had always been something about Andre. How he carried himself. How he presented himself. And how he acted around clients and staff. Always a professional. There were only a handful of people who ever saw the other side of Andre and Nellie was one of them.

Even so, she'd been shocked—horrified—at the footage which had mysteriously appeared on a USB and into Andre's hands. On the surface it was innocent enough, a man and a woman on a romantic walk through a private garden. Except the man—who Nellie recognised—was married to someone else. And their conversation was one likely to destroy that marriage.

Nellie had always known Andre's business was his only priority, but this went too far. Whatever he planned to do with the USB would harm innocent people.

Nellie clicked around the site. She looked for her own profile page...gone. Not even a mention of her as a past employee or any reference to the work she'd done. Instead, there was a page for a much younger woman, perhaps twenty-one or so, but the likeness to the Nellie she used to be was unmistakable. And confronting. The 'about' information was nothing much. Fluff about her degree in marketing and graphic design. She must have done a double degree.

Good for you. Now, leave while you can.

There was a spiel about how excited she was to join the firm and the size of the footsteps to follow so somehow, she knew her predecessor was responsible for a great deal of the success of the firm. Nellie didn't know whether to throw up or feel sad. She did neither, merely breaking off another row of chocolate.

She yawned as she did a search for local tradespeople. There were plenty in Armidale and Tamworth but would they travel this far? A Bindarra Creek listing popped up. Ryan Rossiter looked as if he had access to a range of trades. Nellie jotted his mobile number down as she yawned again. She re-wrapped the remains of the chocolate and put it in with the breakfast and lunch items, closed the laptop, and turned off the phone.

Once again it was sunlight stirring Nellie from her sleep. This time though, she woke slowly, tucking her head under the sheets for a while in a state of half-slumber, stretching her toes into the cooler parts of the bed and enjoying the comfort of a new mattress. But hunger, and the need to visit the bathroom, forced her up before she could fall back asleep.

She really needed a shower. This was now her third day without one. Before dressing she part-filled the sink with water from her drinking supply and washed herself the best she could. Thank goodness it wasn't the middle of winter.

In the kitchen she turned on the phone and made breakfast using the roll, split in half, topped with baked beans.

Electricity had never meant as much. The stove and

oven were both electric not to mention the hot water system. But even when it came on, would she be able to shower or was the water too risky? Picking up her phone and plate, she let herself out of the front door and settled on the top step to eat.

The sun was warm and she shrugged off the light track-suit top. In the past few months, she'd hidden away so much that her normal tan from sea and surf was long gone. The singlet top let the rays heat her skin and it was pure bliss.

Her phone dinged and as she munched on the first half of the bread roll, she stared with suspicion. This was a new phone. Only a handful of people had the number for emergencies. Cory. Two friends who lived in other countries. And her mother. The last of these was through pure necessity. They hadn't got along in...well, forever. But Mum was well into her seventies and living alone and in the few months before Nellie left Manly, they'd managed a few visits which were a bit more than civil. With her dad long dead, Nellie had drifted away from her mother's life until a call out of the blue asking for a dinner date. A shaky start over cocktails ordered by a mother who looked paler and frailer than Nellie remembered, became an evening of reconciliation. To a point. They'd never be close. But Mum had terminal cancer and that meant a lot of soul-searching for Nellie about how she could help.

The first half of breakfast devoured, Nellie picked up the phone. "Is it really after ten?"

No wonder she was so hungry.

The message was from Cory.

> Hey you. I'm worrying now because I
> haven't heard a word in days. I expect you
> are too busy making new friends while you
> host parties on your gorgeous verandah.
> But seriously, let me know you're okay.
> Okay? xx

"I sure am hosting parties on my gorgeous verandah."

Nellie took a few photos, behind and around herself and sent them.

> Not quite the perfect home I expected. A bit
> shell-shocked, actually, about the disrepair.
> And sorry I worried you…I'm doing fine.

That was a lie. Or was it?

The exhaustion was gone. Her stomach was filling. The sun was shining.

"And my neighbour is leaving."

The same 4WD from yesterday slowly cruised past the front of the property and she had no trouble recognising the vehicle. Dark blue, it sat high off the road and had some signage on the doors she couldn't read from here. Maybe he was a tradie? That would be handy. At least her rational side was dominant again and she'd discarded the idea the man had anything to do with her ex-boss. He was probably curious about someone new moving in.

Her phone beeped.

> You cannot live there! Come back to the
> city and we'll sort something out. Seriously,
> Annalise, you are a surf and sea and luxury
> girl, not dust and cobwebs!

Nellie giggled. Cory was wonderful but unrealistic.

But do please come back soon so I can introduce you to my lovely new friend.
Finally think I found 'the one'.

Cory deserved happiness. He'd been alone too long but always said he'd never settle for anything other than an older man and one with an accent. Preferably French.

I've already put new locks on all the doors, have made a bed up, and am getting power today. In a month you won't know the place. And I can't wait to meet 'the one'. Go you. Thanks for caring, Cory. X Nellie

She slid the phone in her shorts pocket and finished breakfast. A couple of interested birds checked her out. Or more likely, her quickly disappearing meal. Was this her future? Local wildlife visiting. Long sunny days. A quiet broken only by birdsong? What she'd said to Cory...about not knowing the place in a month? It suddenly was real. This was her new world and there were worse things in life than doing up an old house and living miles from nowhere. For the first time since she'd stood at the foot of these stairs in a thunderstorm, Nellie had hope.

Once the power was on, Nellie had new problems to solve. She had nothing to cook with and an inspection of all the cupboards in the kitchen only turned up a random selection of plates, glasses, and cutlery. Not even one saucepan. The best news was that the refrigerator started immediately and within an hour was cooling nicely. It had a freezer on the bottom, big enough to store some meals so once she was convinced it would keep running, Nellie again headed to Bindarra Creek.

This time she went straight to the hardware store.

The same gentleman was there and his face creased into a smile. "Let me guess...you had to come back and admire the chainsaws. Or are you more a paint and paint brush fan?"

She found herself grinning. "Not sure about chainsaws yet although I am sure I'll be back in for a mix of power tools. And paint? You will see me often over the next few months. But for now, I hoped you might know who might help me with some repairs? I think I need a carpenter, electrician, and a plumber. Actually, a plumber above all else."

"And why is that?" He opened a book on the counter and began to write down some numbers on a notepad.

"My new house has a water tank which I think have been sitting for a long time. All the taps are working but the water is brown. With bits in it."

"Concrete tanks? Metal?"

"Concrete."

"I can sell you a filter to put onto one tap. See if that helps in the short term but have you had a look inside the tank?"

"Not yet. Where do I look?"

His notes turned into a diagram of a tank. "This bit here is a good place to start. Shine a torch down to make sure there's nothing dead in there. Yeah, I know. But a filter won't help if something climbed in. You might need to let those taps run for a while, longer than you think. The excess water will go into your septic anyway if it was set up right and that'll feed any grass or trees or whatnot. Better than getting ill."

Bottled water it is, then.

"I'll put you onto someone who knows tanks so give him a call and let him know I said he needs to help you out sooner rather than later."

"I don't even know your name."

"Malcolm. Nice to meet you." He extended his hand and Nellie took it.

"Nellie. And thank you."

When she left a few minutes later it was with a tap filter which Malcolm said was returnable if the plumber thought it wasn't suitable. She also had a box of goodies from sink plugs to a saucepan set and more cleaning products. Always more cleaning products. Malcolm carried out the larger items—two brooms, one indoor and one outdoor, plus a rechargeable vacuum.

Next on her list was to do a proper supermarket shop. She filled a trolley with fresh and tinned food, some frozen items, more bottled water and some crockery and cutlery. Coffee in a tin until she could find something more permanent. A couple of bottles of wine. Plenty of everything to keep her going for a while. Packed into several boxes, her shopping looked far more than she'd expected but at least she wouldn't need another trip back in the short term.

As she drove out of the town limits, Nellie put the radio on and sang all the way home.

Chapter Five

"The tank is in good shape, all things considered. But it needs draining and proper cleaning before you start using it for more than flushing the toilet." In bright green overalls with 'Get Tanked' emblazoned on the front, Keith Mills was maybe twenty-five, skinny, with red hair cropped short and a ton of freckles. "I can start the process now and come back tomorrow to give it another flush."

They stood a few feet back from the tank, where a ladder leaned against the side. Keith was the second tradie to arrive this morning after Ryan Rossiter made an appearance straight after breakfast. Using Malcolm's name definitely got help fast.

"That seems like such a waste of water."

"Nah. I'm gonna put a long hose on it and make sure it gets onto some trees and whatnot. Much as it looks gross, I did a test and it won't harm the plant life at all. Not much chance of the fauna touching it as it'll soak into the ground pretty fast." He started off to the front of the house. "Need some stuff from the van."

Nellie caught up. "What about refilling it? I don't think rain is due for a while."

"If you like, I'll arrange a water tanker to come up. He'll have enough for a quarter, maybe a third of that tank and the weather will do the rest." He stopped and gazed up at the roof. "Decent sized area to collect rainfall. I might chuck some new filtration on the main pipe and I'll show you how to clean it."

"You're making this easier than I thought. Well, for me."

He grinned and they began walking again. "Love fixing stuff. Always have. Hope you do 'cos your new home has been empty for years. Rumours are that a ghost drove the last people out."

Nellie stopped in her tracks. "A *what*?"

"Ghost. Nobody has lived here for long. Most recent were renters who stayed for a few months then disappeared."

"Wait...the *renters* disappeared?"

By now Keith was at the back of his van. "Not in a spooky sense. But they packed up and left without paying their rent and quite a few tradies were burned as well. My dad was one back then and had done work on the roof which is why I know how good it is."

"It has some leaks."

He dragged a coiled hose out and tossed it on the ground. "Would be where he stopped. Landlord didn't want to pay up because the rent was months overdue."

So not a ghost at all. Just bad tenants and worse landlord.

Nellie took a look at the house. She'd checked the photos she'd been originally sent and had no doubt they were of this place but with some expert photoshopping involved. If she'd not been so desperate to buy, she would have picked up the small signs.

"Do you know who built it?"

Keith shook his head. "Before my time but there'll be plenty of folk around who do. You should visit Gigi's."

I really need to get my hearing checked.

He noticed her confused expression. "Yeah, it is a funny little shop on the main road. Bit of everything in there, including old local photographs and paintings. Only open a couple of days a week but worth a look."

"By main road you mean in Bindarra Creek?" Nellie picked up a tool bag as Keith heaved the hose over a shoulder.

"Ta. No, Glenmeer. Just over the bridge there's a few shops and stuff."

As she followed Keith around the house, Nellie couldn't remember seeing anything called Gigi's. But now she was curious. Just who was Gigi? And did she know anything about a ghost?

The next few days were non-stop tradespeople in and out. Keith had her tank cleaned and refilled with enough water to keep her going until winter. He'd brought his dad along the last time. A man of few words, he'd been happy to accept a glass of apple juice and refused to take payment after climbing up and finishing the sealing of the roof. Once Keith wrote out his invoice, with a generous timeframe to pay, Nellie added a note to herself to increase it to cover his dad's time and expertise. She believed in paying her way, no matter what.

Thanks to Ryan Rossiter arranging sub-contractors, she had brand new front steps, strong and nice to look at, being a lovely local timber. Internally, the wiring passed inspection after a number of power points and light switches were replaced. A few holes in the ceiling and some walls were freshly plastered, ready for painting. And there were new security screens on all three doors so she could have the house open in the heat yet feel safe. It was unbelievable the change of just a few days.

My house is becoming a home.

She wandered down toward the front of the property as the last of the tradies left for the final time—at least for the time being. The afternoon was humid and the air almost crackling with the chance of a storm. The heady scent of eucalypt and acacia mingled pleasantly with the heat.

Ahead of her, the tradie's ute turned onto the road then stopped as another vehicle pulled up beside it from the other direction. Her neighbour, apparently stopping for a chat.

Not ready to do a meet and greet, Nellie diverted off the driveway. She wound her way between towering trees and all kinds of bushes she had yet to educate herself about, stopping to admire wildflowers growing through cracks in the shady ground. As the slope increased, she gazed back toward the road. There was little to see as the foliage did a good job of screening it.

The less the casual observer can see of my place the better.

Somewhere nearby was running water and Nellie followed the sound. She was behind her house now and closer—at an estimate—to the next door property than she'd been before. A simple wire and post fence confirmed she'd reached the side of her acreage. Her house was quite visible from this point.

Was this where the white flash came from?

Nellie continued along the fence line until it ended at a thicker post. Just beyond, a group of pinkish boulders against a steeply rising hill formed a kind of tiny waterfall as water pooled at the top then trickled down to another pool, overflowing to become a narrow and shallow spring.

"How wonderful." Nellie cupped her palms together and held them beneath the falling water then quickly drank. So cool and incredibly sweet. She adjusted her stance to move a little closer and held her hands out again.

"Don't move!"

Nellie froze.

It was a man's voice. Not Andre. Not Spence. A deep, stern voice behind her.

"I'm only—"

"Stay still. Whatever you do, don't move your feet, or make any sudden hand gestures."

The voice was closer.

Why couldn't she move her feet? Casting her eyes down, her heart almost gave out. Something slid slowly beside her left foot which was on dry grass. A long, narrow body with a fluid motion and a pattern and no legs.

"It'll move on without harming you if you don't challenge it."

Challenge a snake? Are you out of your mind? I couldn't challenge an ant right now.

Sparks flew up and down her spine and her legs had no feeling. Words wanted to come out...a scream wanted to, but her throat had closed in.

"You're okay." The voice was much closer. Not stern. Calming. "Another few seconds and you'll be right to move back."

I'm selling and moving to another city. Any city. Andre is less frightening.

Warm hands clasped her shoulders.

"Take a step back now."

Nellie tried. Nothing worked. But her head managed to shake.

The fingers touching her skin tightened a little.

"The snake is well on its way. It was just passing through and you happened to be in its path. You almost stepped on it which might have resulted in a nasty bite."

Whoever he was, he was right behind her. His breath touched her neck, tingling her skin. "Trust me. Step back."

She did. Right into a body. For just an instant, he kept hold of her shoulders and leaned close to her ear, "You're quite safe."

Nellie still didn't want to move but now it was because she was in some kind of a haze of mind and body. It must be a reaction to the shock. To the fight-flight-freeze response of which freeze had won. Now she was heating up. Pleasantly. All over.

Horrified at herself, Nellie spun around and stepped away, although in the other direction to the one the snake took. She was still close to him...to the man who'd taken the time to stop her being bitten. And been incredibly nice about it. He had the warmest brown eyes she'd ever seen.

"I'm quite alright." Heat rushed to her face at the sharp tone of voice she'd used.

Good grief, he just helped you.

He raised one eyebrow and crossed his arms. Which accentuated his broad shoulders. This was getting worse by the minute. Nellie remembered her manners and softened her tone.

"Thank you. I just got a fright. Snakes aren't my...thing."

"They probably think people aren't their thing either. Just a case of keeping an eye out and letting them go where they want."

Although he made a good point, it didn't help.

She lifted her chin. "I'll be more careful. Thank you again."

You can go now. Before I make more of an idiot of myself.

He didn't get the memo. "I'm Kane. Kane Maxwell. Seems we're neighbours."

Kane wore a white T-shirt, shorts, and heavy, lace-up boots. He was tanned, tall, and about her age. And he still looked at her as if he was trying to work her out. Well, plenty of men had tried that before him and not even one ever succeeded.

"So, it seems. I'm An... I'm Nellie Sinclair." She shoved her right hand in his direction.

He took it. "Nice to meet you, An-Nellie." Little lines crinkled around his eyes.

Are you laughing at me?

If he hadn't saved her from stepping on a snake, she'd turn and walk away. Her new life needed to be safe and private. It wouldn't be difficult, surely, to pretend he didn't exist and live out her life on her side of the fence. Would it?

Kane had obviously moved on. He gestured at the boulders. "The stream flows down from Akuna River which you've probably crossed a number of times in its various incarnations. When we get big storms, like the other night, this tiny waterfall becomes something quite beautiful to behold."

His smile was contagious and as she turned to look back at the waterfall, the negative feelings drained away. The water sparkled in the late afternoon sunlight. Dragonflies hovered above the top pool.

"Pretty beautiful right now," she murmured.

"You've bought the old place?"

"Yes."

"Lots of work."

Nellie drew herself to her full height and smiled at him. Her fake, 'I'll be polite to get rid of you' one, but a smile, nevertheless. "I love hard work."

"That's good. I'll see you around, An-Nellie."

Before she could say a word, Kane Maxwell walked away. He skirted around the end post of the fence line and was quickly lost among the trees on his property.

"That went well." After taking a deep breath to centre herself and a quick glance at the ground for any moving creatures, Nellie headed back to her own house. She'd had quite enough peopling for one day.

Chapter Six

Kane's house was built almost at the same time as his new neighbour's and by the same builder. Both were clad in weatherboard with tin roofs and wrap-around verandahs. And that was where the similarities ended.

He'd bought the property a couple of years ago and with help from Blair—before he'd moved to Sydney—had turned what was a nice but ageing building into a more than comfortable home. Because he loved to cook, he'd spent more time and money on the kitchen than he'd planned but the result was exactly what he'd wanted. Classically old-fashioned appliances with modern functionality. Double sink. Huge pantry. Lots of cupboards and counter space. It was one of his favourite parts of the house but this afternoon he found himself standing in the middle of the kitchen without any clue why he was there.

He poured a glass of water and carried it through the house down the wide hallway with its deep-toned floorboards and timber panelling. Rooms came off from either side. Bedrooms—not all renovated yet, two bathrooms, a formal lounge room which went through to an elegant dining room, then the casual living space at the front. This was opposite his own bedroom and both looked out to the serenity of the bushland through the large windows he'd installed.

The verandah was his destination. This was his other favourite area. Depending upon the time of day and the weather, he'd choose the front or back or a side to relax. All had seating of different kinds and for cooler nights, a large patio heater could be moved to any spot.

Kane stopped at the corner to the right of the door. In an hour the sun would set and long shadows creep toward the house as it slowly dropped behind the canopy. Half a dozen kangaroos grazed on grass made green by his filtered grey water and occasional overnight rain. There was no better life he could have made for himself and he was content.

Over at the house next door, a couple of lights were on. He'd not stepped foot in the place since inspecting it before buying this house but the disrepair was clear in his mind. Holes in walls and the ceiling. Unstable steps and decking. A kitchen with broken cupboards and oddly, an almost new fridge. Even the rank smell of damp carpet lingered if he thought too hard. It was a big job to take on and even with his brother around to help, Kane wouldn't have bought that property.

"Who are you, An-Nellie?"

Something didn't add up about the serious young woman with startling blue eyes. He wasn't one to touch another person without permission, not someone he knew let alone a complete stranger with her back to him. Heck, he hadn't even planned on interrupting what was obviously a happy moment with her hands in the waterfall and her body relaxed. It would have been different had he not seen the snake so close to her feet. She was only wearing runners and with shorts rather than jeans or the like, she wouldn't have stood a chance had the worst happened. His only thought was to stop her from moving.

And it had worked. But scared her half to death.

She was so rigid, so frozen in place from his sudden warning that he'd been compelled to offer something tangible and safe. Firm hands to reassure her someone was watching with her until the snake left. What he hadn't expected was for her to back into his chest. And stay there. She had no idea who he was and for some reason he couldn't explain, he'd been overwhelmed with a need to protect her.

As if she needs protection from a stranger.

It was a response to the moment. Adrenaline, thanks to the danger she was in. And it was his problem because she'd then made it clear that while she appreciated him warning her of the snake's presence, she wasn't about to become his best pal.

No typical small-town friendliness.

Not a neighbourly conversation.

So where did Nellie Sinclair come from?

"So it seems. I'm An... I'm Nellie Sinclair."

An...who? Ann. Annette. Annabelle? But quickly changed to Nellie.

Blair's fancy SUV powered up the driveway and stopped alongside the verandah. "I thought I'd cook tonight."

With the window down, the most delectable smell wafted out.

"Cook?" Kane grinned.

"Pizza. Made them myself."

"In that case go and park and I'll get out the expensive silver."

The SUV moved out of sight.

Kane's eyes were drawn back to the other house. "Who are you?"

"The garlic bread was free with the two pizzas."

Blair acted as if he'd got the deal of the decade and was proud of himself for bringing food home. Cooking wasn't his thing so much. He lived at Bondi Beach in Sydney and admitted to eating out more than at home. But he had a busy life, being a sports physiotherapist for a premier football team. At least for another season.

"How's Miranda?" Kane helped himself to a slice of deliciousness covered in roasted pumpkin, feta cheese, and spinach.

"Busy. She started back at work and the shop has gone crazy again. Not just for grooming bookings but the shop itself. I have no idea how she'll ever cope without me."

Blair had a huge smile as he tore off some garlic bread. He'd spent the week before Christmas helping Miranda in her new grooming salon and pet supplies shop after she'd hurt her ankle in a fall. In Kane's opinion, no couple was better suited but it had taken that week of working together for them to see it.

"She managed before. If anything, Miranda is probably counting down the days until you leave again. I know I am."

Almost coughing on the garlic bread, Blair glared at his brother until he worked out he was being teased. It wasn't as much fun lately getting a rise from him. Love and all that.

I'll ease up on you, buddy. For now.

"I met our new neighbour."

That got Blair's attention.

"She almost stepped on a brown snake up at the boulders."

"Not the best introduction to our local wildlife," Blair said. "What's she like?"

"Bit hard to tell. The snake gave her a fright and she wasn't inclined to have a long conversation afterwards. Doubt if she's had much to do with country life given she was wandering around up there in runners."

"Hope she learns fast. So, she's from Sydney, or further afield?" Blair helped himself to more pizza.

"No idea."

"Well, is she on her own? Old or young? Married? Kids?"

It would never have occurred to Kane to ask a stranger such questions. Blair on the other hand would have her life story by now.

"She's between my age and yours."

"And the rest?"

Kane shrugged and bit into pizza. Nellie hadn't worn a wedding or engagement ring. No rings at all, not even earrings. She'd had a gold chain around her neck with some kind of long pendant. And her hair smelled nice.

He wasn't about to share any more about Nellie and had no idea where that thought came from. Tiredness. Too many days trekking through bushland and nights with half an eye open over his clients.

His phone beeped a message which he ignored.

"Might be important," Blair said with a pointed look at the phone.

"Then they'll call."

"It might be Mum or Dad."

With an exaggerated sigh, Kane reached for the phone. "You haven't changed from those trips in the car as kids where every two minutes it was 'are we there?' or 'I'm hungry'."

"Or bored. Or need a toilet break. Or there's a Macca's ahead. Can we stop?"

"And then the tears when we didn't." Kane grinned.

"Yeah, you used to cry about it a lot."

Kane opened the message, read it, and placed the phone face down on the table.

You've got to be kidding me.

Rather than answer the obvious question on his brother's face, Kane took the remaining piece of garlic bread and chewed. He should have done what he wanted and ignored the message until tomorrow. Or never.

"I'm guessing that's not our parents?"

"Nup."

"No friend in urgent need of help?" Blair asked.

"Not even close."

"I know. The new neighbour. Smelled the pizza and wants to know if we can deliver. Actually, we should take some over. Kinda nice thing to do."

"There are two pieces left, dude." Kane said. "Seems stingy. Besides, how would Nellie know my number?"

Blair's eyes lit up. "*Nellie.* You left out that you know her name. What else did you leave out?"

"I'm going to leave you outside and lock the doors."

The phone beeped again and Kane pushed it further away.

"What's wrong, Kane? All joking aside, who is messaging you?"

"I fancy a glass of wine. Care to join?" Kane was on his feet and at the cupboard before Blair could answer. He took out two glasses and then selected a bottle of Hunter Valley red. For a couple of minutes, he focussed on opening the bottle and pouring the wine, then handed one to his brother. "The message came from a client. I had some ... issues with her on a trip. We were supposed to pitch tents but the storm was heading in fast so I offered her the choice of rebooking or a refund. She made a different suggestion."

"I'm sorry, what kind of suggestion? And cheers." Blair held out his glass and they tapped them together with a clink.

Kane took a long sip. This had better not become a problem. He sat again and reached for his phone. A second message from her.

"She suggested we share the back of the 4WD. And not for the sake of taking cover."

"Oh my gosh." Blair's expression was comical in its shock. "Who even does that?"

"Right. But this was a person whose online booking stated she was an experienced bushwalker who loved camping. Yet, at the first sign of getting her feet wet she asked me to carry her."

"Say what? Carry her, where exactly? And why is she sending you messages?"

Opening the app, Kane read them aloud. "Such a disappointment we didn't get our night out under the stars. Shall we try again? I'll bring the bubbly." He moved to the second message. "Me again. The forecast for tomorrow night is perfect. Can't wait to see you."

"And you had never met her before the camping trip?"

"Never. She booked online and we had a brief phone call to confirm some details. I recall her saying she lives in Armadale and comes up here to visit her mother. That is the sum of my knowledge of Caryn Corday."

And I'd like it to be all I ever know.

There was something uncomfortable about the woman.

"This has firmed up my thinking about limiting the overnight trips to multiple clients. No singles." Kane stood. "I'm going to update my website and that will take the rest of the evening."

"What about the messages? Any idea how to respond?"

"Refund. I'd wanted to do that on the spot but she asked me to wait until she knew when she'd be back up. But I'll do it now and send an email from my business to let her know."

That should then be the end of it. He'd change his policies. Refund the money. Move on.

Chapter Seven

Nellie woke in a cold sweat, bolt upright with her top sheet cast aside.

Her breath came fast despite her limbs feeling paralysed by the remnants of an awful dream. It was dark outside and the lack of curtains accentuated morbid thoughts of being pursued and cornered. And an uncanny sensation that a light had shone into the room.

You're safe. New home. New town. Nobody bad knows you're here.

She repeated it until the tingling in her legs signalled mobility.

As she swung her feet out of the bed, Nellie reached for her dressing gown, trying to slide into her slippers at the same time. By the time she'd tied the sash around a waist she'd noticed was thinner than it had ever been, she was wide awake and the dream receded.

Without turning on any lights, she went to the kitchen and opened the fridge, blinking at the sudden brightness. The fridge was the one good, workable part of the house and it was stocked up with a range of fresh produce. If only the oven would work but at least the stove top did. There was a list of appliances to replace. Nellie took a bottle of water and closed the door. After sitting at the table, she twisted the top and sipped.

What had brought on such a frightening dream out of the blue?

This was her third week here. Life was settling into a routine of progressively removing rubbish, dragging out carpet and derelict furniture combined with slowly working on making rooms more liveable. There was a lot of work ahead and she'd already decided to pace herself. Not every day needed to be about ripping out old carpet or loading up yet another skip bin for collection but she'd not left the property in days doing exactly that.

What she did need was to buy decent boots to wear outside instead of runners. Almost standing on a brown snake—she'd researched what kind it was which almost stopped her heart again knowing how high the risk was that day—had made her extra cautious. Had it not been for Kane Maxwell, she might be in hospital. Or worse.

Her neighbour hadn't made any more appearances but she was getting used to his 4WD leaving early, even before dawn some days, and returning late in the afternoon. There was a second car which came in and out at different times. An Audi SUV. Probably his wife or girlfriend. The thought of there being a woman in Kane's life made her squirm a bit at her silly response that day to his touch and his calm voice.

And those eyes.

Deciding that was enough of her rambling thoughts, and having no desire to try sleeping again, Nellie showered and dressed. While water heated on the stove for coffee, Nellie made a new list.

- Kettle
- Toaster
- Microwave
- Look at ovens (measure space first)
- Look at washing machines

The last two items were getting urgent. She'd found a DIY laundry in Bindarra Creek and twice taken loads of washing there, using each visit to top up her shopping. It wasn't a long-term solution.

Coffee made, she searched for local white goods shops on her laptop. Although she could probably pick up some of the smaller items locally, there were no businesses selling the big appliances in Bindarra Creek. That left her with a trip to Tamworth and if she was going so far, she'd try to buy as much for the house as possible in one go. She transferred some money from her secondary bank account to one she could access using her debit card.

Money was the least of her worries. Her Manly apartment sold quickly and not only covered the purchase of this property, but the next year of living expenses. She didn't need to find a job for a while which was good because she was at a loss of what to do.

She puzzled over it while cooking an omelette. Her whole working life she'd been a graphic designer.

A good one.

Creating something wonderful from an idea gave her a thrill and was one of the reasons she'd never spent time worrying about relationships. Her work fulfilled her. That and the beach. And while she couldn't change not having a beach anywhere close, perhaps there was a way to continue in her chosen profession.

Nellie took her plate outside and sat on the front steps, as she'd become accustomed to doing as the sun rose. It came from the back corner of the property, preceded by birdsong and chatter. Magpies warbled and cockatoos screeched while a family of kookaburras, Nellie had recently spied, broke into their characteristic laughter.

"Come to the country. It will be quiet. Peaceful." She laughed.

Before going inside, she watered the pot she'd bought on impulse from the hardware store and placed at the top of the steps. Once she'd sorted the worst of the problems with the house out, Nellie intended to create lots of vegetable gardens. For now, this pot with rosemary and basil and oregano would have to do and the gorgeous scent of the young herbs intensified with the water. But the basil looked a little pale, so she dragged the pot from the left side of the steps to the right so it might get a little more sunshine.

"Look at me. Instead of fancy smashed avocado toast on the Esplanade, I'm encouraging herbs to grow for my omelettes. Next up, it'll be chickens running around for free-range eggs."

Which sounds perfect.

When Nellie first moved into her Manly apartment, there'd been little for her to do thanks to its existing Bohemian style which she quite liked. It was gifted to her by her father who'd lived there until moving to Spain with his latest wife and it was the only good thing he'd done for her. That, and switching to the name he'd given her. Annalise Fontaine. Its fanciness appealed to her sense of humour. Before then, she'd gone by her mother's surname, Sinclair.

It was complicated.

In fact, both of her parents were complicated.

Although she spent her childhood with her mother, things got so bad during the last year of high school that she moved in with her dad. Such an eye opener, living with a man she had such intermittent memories of. It was worth the hour of travel each way to school for the return to Manly. Mum lived inland and discovering the lifestyle...and the beach, was enough to keep Nellie with her father despite his flaws.

Straight into a design degree after school, Nellie's needs changed. No longer a kid, she began to judge her parents—perhaps harshly—for their respective faults. Mostly, for their offhand approach to raising a child. With the judgement came a list of demands and to her surprise, her father was willing to agree to each of them.

A regular deposit into her bank account to cover her day-to-day expenses.

The freedom to stay out late when she wanted without any questions.

No comments about anyone she dated.

Looking back, Nellie knew she had pushed the boundaries but it hadn't been in order to misbehave. She knew what to do. She rarely dated. She didn't need her father's money because she had a part-time job on Manly Pier. And the late nights were often spent at friends' houses studying. But she'd learned to ask for what she wanted which revealed exactly how lax her father was when it came to raising a child.

Selling the apartment and her car had hurt.

If Andre hadn't almost caught her that night...

But within an hour of her escape, he'd phoned and left messages which chilled her. Return the USB or her life wouldn't be worth living. He gave her until dawn or he'd be at her apartment and she would regret stealing from him.

She'd packed a couple of suitcases before fear sent her fleeing to the relative safety of a series of motels. She'd returned days later—after checking his whereabouts—to collect the most important of her possessions and once to take a real estate agent through. Then she'd handed over the keys and never looked back.

She pulled into the carpark of a large homemaker's centre in Tamworth and parked.

There'd been more threats after she contacted him to try to make sense of it all. Why was he going to blackmail Carlo Bianchi? The answers made no sense and then the anger poured out of him until she'd hung up, tears streaming down her face and fear in her heart. He promised to use his connections in the government and police force to hunt her down and not just for the purpose of retrieving the USB.

With only Cory to trust, Nellie had faced the possibility she was unsafe and probably would be for a long time. She'd hide where he'd never find her and eventually, he'd give up looking. Give up on his need to ruin Carlo Bianchi. He had to if there was no video to use as leverage.

In the carpark, Nellie still held onto the steering wheel, her knuckles white. The time was approaching for her to get help resolving this. Otherwise, how would she ever move on?

Nellie pulled up close to the front steps. She had boxes and bags to take inside and the less distance to carry them, the better. Her shopping trip was a success and tomorrow, a delivery van would bring new whitegoods. Her smaller purchases were better off coming in the car.

No point waiting until tomorrow!

Excitement bubbled away with each load up the stairs. She left the front doors open and carried an armful at a time into the house. The microwave took a bit of juggling but she got it onto the kitchen table and grabbed some water before going back for the most important box.

She'd found a top-quality office printer. Not offset commercial quality but the closest thing to it. It was a sign. The details were to be determined but Nellie was filled with ideas of how to build a new business for herself.

"Hello? Nellie?"

Kane Maxwell stood on the doorstep, looking back down the driveway. Or at her car.

"There isn't another snake, is there?" Maybe if she tried to be funny, she could create a façade of friendliness she didn't feel.

He turned and his smile did something ridiculous to her legs. Clearly there was no reptile slithering around to excuse the response this time.

"Haven't seen one since the other week."

She stepped past him, onto the verandah, unwilling to invite him in. Nobody was coming into the house until she knew she was safe. "Well, that's good to hear. I'm just emptying my car if you don't mind..."

"Happy to help." Kane sprinted down the stairs.

"I didn't mean you needed to help." She followed. "That is really heavy."

He was halfway into the back of the SUV, slowly dragging the printer box out. "Where would you like this?"

"Really, Kane?" She put her hand on his arm and immediately regretted touching him when sparks lit up her fingertips. When he glanced at her, she lifted her hand. "I'm fine to manage it. I just meant I have a lot to do."

"Then I'll get out of your hair. Living room? Or have you set up an office?" He lifted the box with no effort and tilted his head while he waited for instructions.

"Oh, on the verandah."

He climbed the stairs then stopped, the box in his arms. "I'm not going to barge in uninvited but if you'd like me to carry it in, I don't mind."

Why am I being so difficult?

"Just inside the door, then. Thank you. I...um, I haven't decided where to put it yet."

Through the open door, Kane stopped again as he lowered the box gently and pushed it to one side.

"Shouldn't be in the way there." He stepped outside straight away. "There is a reason for my dropping in."

Swatting a fly away from her face, Nellie closed the screen door. Hopefully not too many of the pests had gone inside. Kane had moved partway down the steps and turned to face her but her eyes drifted to the pot of herbs. Something was different about it.

"My brother, Blair, is heading back to the city soon and we're having a barbeque to celebrate him leaving."

To celebrate?

Kane was grinning. "No annoying younger siblings? Anyway, his girlfriend and her grandfather are coming over so just a small group. You're most welcome to join us. Give you a chance to meet some of the strange locals and let someone else cook for you."

About to refuse, she realised what was wrong with the pot and her blood turned to ice.

"Did you happen to move this?" There was a small trail of dirt from where she'd left the pot this morning. "How on earth had it got back to its original spot?"

"The pot? Nope. Do you need it moved? The basil could use more sun on it."

Her eyes shot to his face, evaluating his expression, searching for a lie. She was good at reading people. Kane wasn't lying. Sheer panic coursed through her and she pulled her car keys from a pocket.

"Er, I need to move my car. Yes. Can you put the pot on the other side? Just there?" She pointed to where she'd left it this morning. "I'll be right back."

They passed on the steps, arms brushing and she almost fell as she tried to avoid contact. Thank goodness, he didn't notice. She shut the boot and jumped into the driver's seat.

Please don't leave yet.

There was nobody to trust, but her instincts insisted Kane wasn't a threat. Except to her heightened senses. After parking and locking the car, Nellie ran to the front of the house, relieved Kane was waiting at the bottom of the steps. At least she could get into the house and lock herself there before he'd gone too far.

"You okay?"

How could she tell a perfect stranger she believed somebody had been on her property and moved a pot? How could she say she was frightened without sounding crazy? She forced a smile. "Just out of breath. Thanks for moving the pot. Goodbye."

As she reached the front door, his low laughter followed her and she glanced back.

"Goodbye, Nellie. Seven onwards tonight. Barbeque. No need to bring anything."

He waved and walked away and she flung herself inside, locking the screen door and staring at his disappearing back. She couldn't possibly go to his house. Meet people. Socialise.

Someone had been here. At her house.

Chapter Eight

Nellie Sinclair was hiding something.

Kane got to the end of the driveway before looking back.

She'd done a good job of covering it up but her eyes gave away a fearfulness which tugged at him. Nobody should be afraid of their own shadow.

The front door was closed now. He'd heard both the security screen door and main door lock behind him. He waited for a few minutes, scanning the grounds...or as much as he could see through the bush. There were no movements other than birds in the trees and on the ground. Not even kangaroos. And no humans. He started for home.

Is it just the remoteness? One neighbour within miles?

First, she'd hidden behind a tree when he'd driven past, just after she'd moved in.

Then, she'd corrected herself when saying her name the first time they met. An-what? Most likely Nellie was short for another name but why not say so? Lots of people shortened their real name.

And just now she'd gone white when she stared at the pot of herbs.

"Did you happen to move this?" Her tone of voice when she'd asked wasn't accusatory. No, he got the feeling she'd hoped for an affirmative answer. There'd been some crumbs of soil leading to the opposite side of the steps where he'd moved it to while she parked her car. But why would anyone move a fairly heavy pot a couple of metres?

Blair's SUV drew up beside him, passenger window wound down as he paced Kane's walk. "Lift?"

"Dunno. Mum taught me not to get into cars with strangers and you look kind of creepy. Might take my chances with the wildlife."

"Just saw a huge crocodile head this way but suit yourself."

"A croc so far south and inland is newsworthy."

"Might have been a cow." Blair began to raise the window. "Or a scary client."

He drove off, turning into the driveway a few metres along. By the time Kane reached his house, the SUV was parked across the steps and Blair was lugging bags of shopping to the top of the stairs.

"Déjà vu."

Kane took a handful of bags and followed.

"Why déjà vu?" Blair juggled bags while searching for the key to the door.

"Just helped our neighbour carry a box into her place. Had her car exactly where yours is but at least she doesn't have nice grass out the front to risk being ruined by tyres."

Blair snorted. "You call that grass nice?"

"It is green."

"It is woeful. Gimme a minute." The door swung open and Blair went straight through to the kitchen. "I think I got everything. Do you want me to check the gas cylinder on the barbeque?"

"Yes. And give the grills a bit of a polish. I left it clean but haven't fired it up for a while."

"Done. Give me ten to change and I'll find a bucket." Blair stopped at the doorway. "Is our mystery neighbour joining us?"

"Unsure. But we'll prep as if she is and anything spare can be leftovers."

Looking at the bags of shopping, Kane had a feeling there'd be plenty left over even if another ten guests fronted. This was going to be fun.

"You do put on a good feed, son." Pop Layton helped himself to a cracker with cheese, relish, and caramelised onion. "Never can get enough to eat at my age."

Blair patted Pop on the back. "At any age."

Kane had prepped for the barbeque while Blair tidied and got tables and chairs.

Salads, a selection of crackers with various toppings, a few dips—including Kane's favourite warm cheesy garlic dip inside a cob loaf—and huge potatoes already cooking wrapped up in foil. There was a selection of fish he'd caught earlier and both veg and meat kebabs ready to toss on the grill.

They were outside where a long trestle table held most of the offerings and two buckets of ice contained soft drinks, wine, and beer. Pop was designated driver so that his granddaughter Miranda could enjoy a glass of wine if she wished.

"You were welcome to bring Beryl," Blair said. "Or is she still visiting family?"

Pop nodded. "New grandchild just arrived, so she's

spending some time helping out. I know she wanted to give you a hug before you left so I'll have to do it for her." He grinned and pretended to go after Blair with his arms wide open. Blair ducked and hid behind Miranda, who'd stepped through the back door carrying the last of the salads.

"Blair, seriously? You should take Pop to Sydney with you."

After planting a kiss on her cheek, Blair took the bowl from her hands and deposited it on the table. "I would struggle to keep up with him. Besides, who would look after you?"

Miranda shot him a glare. Kane found it funny and cute.

Blair and Miranda were best friends all through high school and kept in touch when he went to university in other towns. Then a year or so ago, Blair landed his dream job as a sports physiotherapist at a premier football club in Sydney. Miranda, meanwhile, opened her grooming salon and retail pet supplies shop attached to a house she'd built on Pop's property. All in all, both were following their dreams and doing well.

When an accident forced them together around Christmas, among the worries and wonders of the season, they'd discovered what their loved ones already knew. A perfect match. But even the best matches needed time to adjust and Blair obviously believed Miranda needed him around to help a lot more than she did. One more year apart then they were determined to be together.

And they will succeed.

Kane was proud of his little brother.

"So, I've given Tangles my private hotline to call if he has any concerns," Blair said.

On the other hand...

Miranda scooped up a piece of tomato and threw it at Blair. He avoided it. Just.

Pop laughed.

Tangles—who was Miranda's Labrador—barked.

But not at the nonsense going on out here.

Head and tail high, the dog disappeared around the verandah.

"Dude, watch the potatoes." Kane instructed his brother.

"Can't see any. Only these lumps of foil."

Kane left the laughter behind him, following Tangles around the house. Although it was still light, he'd put on the lights. Just in case. The way Nellie had rushed into her house and locked herself in gave him little hope she'd accept his invitation. But her voice stopped him before he reached the last corner.

"Aren't you the most gorgeous creature ever!"

The heavy thumping of Tangles's tail evidenced his agreement and when Kane looked around the corner, the dog was lying on his side letting Nellie rub his chest. He was clearly smitten with her.

"How I wish I had a dog like you. Would you like to run away and live with me? Two runaways together." She sat on the top step, her tone conspiratorial. "We could hang out a lot and I don't mind if you want to sleep on the bed. You are in such beautiful shape so maybe we won't share a lot of food though."

Two runaways?

Nellie's hair was pulled back in a bun and her face was alight with happiness as she and Tangles made friends.

Not wanting to startle her, Kane took a couple of steps back out of sight, then whistled. "Tangles, where did you go?" He stepped loudly on the deck and by the time he made what Nellie would believe was his first appearance, she was on her feet. "Ah, that's where he went. Must have heard you."

"His name is Tangles? Like the cricketer?"

"Yup. And you are going to get on very well with the person who named him."

The smile dropped from her lips and she glanced down the steps.

"Come and meet everyone."

She fidgeted from foot to foot—which were clad in decent lace-up walking boots and ran her hands down the side of her jeans. "Actually, maybe I shouldn't—"

"I'm happy you're here. There's way too much food for four people and probably too much for five, but you are welcome to stay."

Her eyes were huge as doubt and some other conflict went back and forth over her features. Tangles sat up and leaned against her and Nellie's fingers scratched the top of his head.

How do I make you feel safe and welcome?

"Oh, there you all are! Hello, Nellie, I'm Miranda and I have to apologise for both my canine and my boyfriend's brother acting as a barrier to you joining me for a glass of wine." Miranda breezed over, hand outstretched. "And before you meet him, I will apologise for my boyfriend...just because."

Nellie's mouth flickered up in a small smile as she shook Miranda's hand.

"So, do you prefer red or white wine? Or bubbles? We have everything because your new neighbour is nothing if not a generous man and amazing caterer." Miranda linked her arm through Nellie's. "I do hope you'll join me for a glass because the rest of them think beer is nicer."

"Wine is fine. White. Actually, anything," Nellie actually laughed and as she passed Kane with Miranda, her smile was sunshine. Ten times over. "And beer is good too."

With that, both women were gone and Tangles trotted after them.

"Should have led with wine, then," Kane muttered.

Kane had to hand it to his guests...they knew how to make someone feel at home. He'd been right about Pop getting on well with Nellie and they'd spent a lot of time swapping stories about cricketing greats. She had a decent knowledge of the game and talked Pop into watching an upcoming women's Big Bash game.

"Kinda prefer the tests," he said.

"But there's nothing like the pace and energy of the T20 matches. If you ever get a chance to see one live...particularly the women's teams...just outstanding."

Kane enjoyed hearing snippets of the conversation as he finished cooking, his eyes drawn to Nellie's animated features time and again. She'd taken a chair beside Pop, and Tangles had dropped himself between them. Every so often she'd reach down to pet the dog with her free hand. The other held the original glass of wine Miranda poured her. She'd only taken a couple of sips by the look of it.

"Are the potatoes ready to put on the table?" Miranda wandered across with a tray. "Everything smells divine."

"They're done. And can you find the sour cream? Blair was cutting up some chives to sprinkle on top and I've not seen the bowl since."

Miranda grinned as she piled potatoes onto the tray with tongs. "I'm glad your attention to detail is rubbing off on him. He might actually start feeding himself at home instead of eating out all the time. Can't be good for him in the long run."

Ah, the sweet strains of new love.

"She's really nice."

"Sorry?"

"Nellie."

"Yes, she is." Kane glanced over at the table where Nellie was helping Pop pour glasses of water and set them by each plate. "Thanks for earlier. She was a bit nervous about meeting everyone."

"Coming through. Don't anyone move...just relocating a little friend." Blair held a broom outstretched ahead of himself with the brush up high. Gripping the end was a huge huntsman spider which began to edge down the handle toward Blair. "Oh no you don't! Going faster!" Breaking into a jog, Blair cleared the entertainment area and vanished between some trees. "Trying to save your life, you hairy interloper."

Pop was laughing aloud but Nellie, whose back was turned to Kane, was rigid. Her shoulders began to shake and Kane dropped the tongs he'd just lifted and stepped around the barbeque. She must be terrified. He couldn't stand it if she burst into tears thanks to a spider in his home.

Nellie's hands went to her face and she turned, but it was her mouth she had covered and when her eyes met Kane's, there was no fear in them. She was struggling to contain her mirth and it made him chuckle. For a second she closed her eyes, and then the flood gates opened and she burst into laughter. Everyone else joined in. Tangles jumped up and went from person to person as if trying to help these silly humans.

Only one person wasn't amused. Blair, broom right way up, stood on the edge of the paved area. "Next time one of you deal with the giant intruder." He frowned. "Put my life at risk, I did. And this is the thanks I get."

Miranda hurried to him and kissed his cheek. "You are my hero, Blair."

He still frowned.

She took the broom and turned to the others. "Do you know that when I had my sprained ankle, Blair insisted on cleaning all the big floor mats I use in the grooming salon? He told me he needed practice to be good at...what did you call it...brooming? That's right, which is how he swept me off my feet."

Miranda squealed as Blair lifted her up, the broom falling with a thud.

"If anyone's hungry..." Kane mentioned.

Chapter Nine

How long, Nellie? How long since you've felt so good?

The decision to accept Kane's invitation was a mixture of curiosity about her neighbour and a strange need to convince herself he wasn't associated with Andre. Being social wasn't even on her radar. But the genuine warmth and welcome from this tight-knit group swept her suspicions away. That and Tangles.

Around the table, the faces belonged to ordinary people who cared about each other.

Pop Layton was a darling. A man who'd seen much in his life and was—he'd mentioned with a sparkle in his eyes —dating again for the first time since his twenties. He adored his granddaughter and Nellie got the impression he'd known Kane and Blair for many years.

Earlier, she'd been ready to leave when Miranda had appeared from nowhere and swept her away from Kane and Tangles. The younger woman had such a kind aura and had quickly settled Nellie next to Pop, introduced them, and brought her a glass of wine.

Blair was funny and a bit of a charmer but his love for

Miranda oozed from every pore and would have been sickly sweet had it not been so honest. He also had a silly side and didn't mind stirring everyone up, especially his brother.

Which brought her to Kane.

He was something of a surprise. His house was beautiful. He cooked like a professional. And he was nice. There wasn't a trace of dishonesty or bravado about him and he tolerated his brother's teasing with a dry sense of humour. It was similar to her own. Add the fact he was good looking and fit and it had her wondering about him. There was no wife. No girlfriend attending tonight or mentioned by anyone. Was he of the same mindset she'd been her whole adult life? Find a job you love and put everything into it.

"Has everyone had enough to eat?" Kane pushed his chair back and stood. "As expected, there are a ton of leftovers so please, everyone take something home."

With all of them carrying plates inside and helping clean up, it didn't take long until the outside area was clear of evidence of the evening. Kane lined up a row of large foil containers for leftovers. "That includes you, Nellie. As long as you can stand eating more of my food." He grinned as he handed her a large spoon. "Don't forget the potato salad. I have too many of the things growing still."

She didn't need a second invitation. Every bit of the meal, from the freshest grilled fish she'd ever tasted through to the range of salads, was delicious.

"So, potatoes grow okay here?" she asked.

"You should see Kane's little market garden," Blair said. "If you're thinking of growing produce, take a look. Has its own water tank, fences to keep the pests out—"

"The four-legged ones," Kane said.

"And lots of companion planting to help manage the flying ones." Blair grinned. "I'm available to write advertising copy for a suitable fee."

"Stick to physio, mate."

"I thought you did pretty well, Blair. Plenty of benefits mentioned in a short space. Just needs a tweak here and there."

The others stopped what they were doing to look at her.

"What? Praise where its due," Nellie said.

Miranda grabbed a magnet off the fridge and pushed it at Nellie. "What do you think of this? First impressions?"

"Oi." Kane shook his head but went back to wrapping up the remains of the fish.

The magnet advertised a business—*Glenmeer Guided Adventures*. The shopfront she'd seen the other day. The background was black with the name in white, capitalised, heavy fonts. The rest of the text was also white and tiny, thanks to the volume.

She handed it back. "I'm guessing this is something you aren't a fan of, Miranda?"

Miranda rolled her eyes. "Good guess. Who can even read something so small?"

Blair took the magnet from her and returned it to the fridge. "Not everyone has an eye for design like you, my sweetie. Better than having nothing to promote a business."

"True. I just know the importance of branding and how much it helped my grooming salon and shop."

Pop dropped onto a chair. "Bit easier branding with cute dogs than white water rafting."

"Yes and no," Nellie said. "Cute puppies will always

catch the consumer's eye but so can a powerful image of nature if an ad is properly constructed."

Why are you all staring at me?

"Sounds like you know what you're talking about, Nellie," Miranda glanced at Kane for some reason. "Are you in advertising?"

She wasn't ready for this conversation. These people had done nothing other than welcome her but she didn't know them. And she was nowhere near a decision on what was a half-baked idea for a future job.

"Would you like another glass of wine? Or coffee?" Kane spoke directly to Nellie and his eyes gave away the fact he'd picked up on her discomfort. He was the perfect host.

She forced a smile. "Actually, I might say goodnight. Meeting you all have been so nice."

Miranda hurried over and gave her a big hug. "Here, take my card so you have my number. And come and visit me anytime. Or Pop."

Tangles flopped against her legs.

"Or Tangles?"

"Especially Tangles."

———

Moonlight made a torch unnecessary along the hard, dirt road between the two properties. Kane had picked up her container of leftovers and said he'd do a special home delivery. Nellie hadn't refused. She wasn't entirely comfortable with her new surroundings and still worried about the herb pot being moved.

They walked without speaking, their boots crunching on the ground.

"Stop for a sec," Kane whispered, one hand on Nellie's

arm.

At first, she didn't know what she was supposed to see but branches at the bottom of a bush began to shake and then a roundish body waddled onto the road. A pair of small eyes glanced at them without changing direction and in a minute, it disappeared into the undergrowth over the road.

Nellie let out a breath. "I can't believe that."

"Never seen a wombat?"

"Well, yes. Of course. But not in the wild. Not...here."

Kane chuckled. "Stand still for long enough and you'll be introduced to a parade of local wildlife."

"As long as they aren't dangerous. Like the snake." She gazed around suspiciously and began to walk. "The wombat wasn't afraid of us."

"Well, it can protect itself and outrun most of us which is why we stopped to let it go about its business. Last thing you want is a bite or being bowled over. I mean, you saw the size of it."

Without meaning too, Nellie moved closer to Kane, her eyes darting from one side of the road to the other. "Next you'll tell me the kangaroos are out to get me."

Kane looked at her, his eyebrows raised. "Okay, how often have you been out in the bush? Or have you moved to a country property with no previous exposure to the environment?"

"No. I mean, no I haven't lived in the bush before. But I've lived in Australia my whole life so how come I didn't know about wombats? They are depicted as cute and cuddly, not some hairy, sabre-toothed bowling ball."

That made Kane laugh but Nellie wasn't amused by any of this.

Have I swapped one kind of danger for another?

They turned into her driveway. Here, with more of a canopy of trees, the moonlight was filtered and Nellie took more care where she stepped.

"So, kangaroos?"

"They'll cohabitate with you but don't approach them. Some of the males get a bit antagonistic if they feel threatened and will inflict damage. I'll send you a link to a good site about local creatures and how to manage interactions."

Laughter drifted across from Kane's house.

"I really enjoyed tonight. You have nice friends and family."

"Even with spiders on brooms?"

She smiled as they reached the bottom of the steps. "Blair is very funny. And sweet."

"Do you want me to check the house?" Kane's expression had sobered.

"What for?"

He glanced up the steps at the pot.

I do. But I can't let you.

"Thanks. But I'm fine to let myself in."

"Okay. Oh, the link to that website." He reached into a pocket and found a card. "My website has a link on it. And that's my personal number in case you ever need to get hold of me."

Nellie smiled as she took the card.

"And Nellie? Thank you for not slamming my fridge magnet. Not that you could have known it was mine. Miranda has a thing about it."

"I guessed it was yours." She went up the first step then turned to look at Kane, who was at eye level. How could such dark brown eyes be so expressive in the low light? She almost forgot what she was going to say. "If *you* asked my opinion, I'd give it."

"Maybe I will one day."

The longer he stood there, the smallest of smiles on his lips, the more Nellie wanted to lean closer to Kane. It had to be the wine and how relaxed and safe she was feeling right now and it was a terrible idea. Relationships were out. Eventually she'd let her guard down but not yet. Not for a long time. And not with her only neighbour.

"Don't forget your home delivery," Kane said, offering her the foil container.

"Right. And thanks again. If I ever get this place sorted, I'll reciprocate."

Good grief, don't make promises!

"Looking forward to it."

Kane stepped back and Nellie took the steps. She couldn't help checking the herb pot was in the right place. It was.

"Goodnight, An-Nellie."

"Very funny. But goodnight, Kane."

She unlocked the door and switched on the hall light. When she went to close it, he was walking away, his hand up in a wave. She clicked it closed and turned the lock, then pulled the chain across.

One by one she turned on every light and checked each room. When she reached the kitchen, she slid the container into the fridge then went back through the house. This time she made sure every window and door were locked, turning off most of the lights again. She left the hall and bedroom and kitchen lights on while she made coffee. For the first time the house had a sense of emptiness.

Being with Kane and Blair, Miranda, and Pop...and Tangles...it had filled up a well of loneliness she didn't know existed. And now, in the emptiness of the house, the well began to leak.

Chapter Ten

Unpacked and set up, the printer was everything Nellie expected.

She'd created business cards, a brochure, and an A5 sized flyer based around a handful of services she could immediately offer. Later in the week she'd drive into Bindarra Creek to make a list of potential clients plus find a printing company able to handle the jobs her printer couldn't. Along with the printer she'd purchased a selection of clever shape cutters and a guillotine.

The printer hummed into action and in minutes, Nellie poured over the brochure.

Nellie's Graphic Design—well, she needed to come up with a better name but for the purpose of testing all of this it would do.

There was a short spiel about herself, and though it was short, it had taken the longest time to write. How on earth to introduce herself to the community without giving away her past?

When Nellie found her new home online, she was compelled to leave the big smoke for a tree change. The natural beauty of the region stirred her soul. With a decade of graphic design, Nellie cannot wait to help you bring your own creative dreams to life.

It wasn't her best work but she'd refine it before letting the general public read the brochure.

"I need to test it, though." Using a control group was always part of any ads she'd designed and if she was to build a business, then she owed the same process to herself.

Using a red pen, she scribbled notes and changed some words then went back to her computer. This time she produced two versions. One with black text on a cream background using gold and burgundy to highlight, and the other using a photo of her front garden with a simple text overlay. Perfect for a test.

There was no point putting it off, not if she was serious about creating a small business.

You don't need to work.

She didn't believe it for a minute. Work-career-fulfil-ment. One led to the next. And there was only so much she could do at a time on the property. Looking ahead, if the house took a year to turn into a home as charming and inviting as Kane's property, what then? Nellie was thirty-two. Hardly retirement age. She was accustomed to hard, challenging work. Thrived on it. And although she believed she could spend years on the land and still have something to do, it didn't replace her need to surround herself with her passion.

The drive to Glenmeer was second nature now and on the far side of the hamlet she pulled into the dirt carpark of a small park which had some swings and a public convenience.

This was the first time she'd stopped and got out of the car. Usually, she was intent on different destinations and only glanced at the handful of shops and businesses here. It was far prettier than she'd noticed and she wandered to the middle of the empty road and took a few photographs with her phone.

The rumble of a motorcycle approaching from the direction of Bindarra Creek interrupted her session and Nellie moved onto the grass verge. As it passed her, the motorcycle slowed and the rider looked her way. A long look. They were dressed in black from head to foot and invisible behind the visor so there was no way for Nellie to identify the rider.

A shiver went up her spine.

In a minute the motorcycle headed over the bridge, the sound of the motor fading as it got further away.

Nellie bit her lip. Somehow, she had to move on from jumping at every shadow. Nobody who would harm her knew where she was. Even her mother didn't know exactly, only having the post office box details she'd paid for in Bindarra Creek. All her mail went there and so far, all she'd received were bills and some real estate correspondence.

The quiet was restored. Nellie was on the right side of the road to visit Kane's shopfront. *Glenmeer Guided Adventures* was a small standalone building in the middle of a large, chain-fenced yard. The ground was hard dirt and a driveway went right around the building. At the back of the yard, a larger shed ran along the length of the property. Kane's 4WD was parked to one side and a huge sliding door was open.

The front door was locked with a sign...*please go to shed.*

She'd not seen Kane since the night of his small party. Well, she had, but only to wave from one verandah to the other—now she knew the right spot to stand to see his house.

84

The strangest sounds emanated from the shed, getting louder as she got closer. Music, thumping—like a hammer —and...singing?

When she stepped inside, the shade was a welcome respite from the growing heat of the day, but the sound hadn't improved. Nellie squinted as her eyes adjusted. On a row of racks were kayaks and canoes. More racks contained camping equipment. And in the middle of the shed, whacking a raft with a mallet, Kane—who wore only a pair of shorts and his habitual hiking boots—sang loudly along with the song from a radio.

If you can call that singing.

But whether he could hold a tune was of little consequence. Nellie's eyes roamed over his muscular back and shoulders. He was fit.

Her heart rate increased.

She couldn't let him find her staring at him like this...

"Nellie?"

Whoops.

Kane put his mallet down and reached for his top which was slung over the back of some piece of machinery. It really didn't help when he pulled it over his head. If anything, it was impossible to avoid looking at his abs. He tucked his top into his shorts and turned off the radio. "Would you like some water? I need some."

Without waiting for an answer, Kane stalked out of the shed in the direction of the small shop. There was a back entry and he waited there, holding open a screen door.

"Oh, thanks. So, you lock the front and leave the back open?" Nellie grinned as she slipped past him into a kitchenette.

"Good point. But so far, everyone follows my note on the front door and comes to the shed." Kane let the screen door close itself and opened a small fridge. "I have filtered water or an energy drink."

"Water please."

Nellie leaned against a counter. Although small, the room was functional with lots of shelving, sink, and the fridge. There was a chest freezer in a corner. And the sweetest thing was flowers in a jar of water.

Kane caught her admiring them. "They grow between the end of the shed and the fence and there are so many I don't think a few are missed." He handed her a glass of water he poured from a jug. "Are you exploring our huge kingdom?"

"Easy to get lost, it is so big. But yes. I've not stepped foot on this vast tract of magical land and was lured by the call of a siren..."

Biting her bottom lip to stop herself, Nellie glanced down. She'd probably offended Kane.

But he laughed. "Siren, huh? Not what Blair would call my singing but I believe in that old adage...you know the one? Sing like nobody is listening." He stepped close to Nellie and held his arms in the position of a waltz. "Dance like nobody is watching."

That urge was back. The one to lean toward him and let his strength envelope her senses.

With a nervous laugh, Nellie lifted her glass. "Clearly, you've never seen my attempts at dancing."

"Well, that's kinda the point I'm making."

A person could get lost in those eyes.

He tilted his head. "So, no dancing today?"

The moment disappeared as he picked up his glass and disappeared through another doorway.

"Come and see the shop."

It was small. A long counter ran almost the length of the

space with a hinged, half-height door at the end. Between the window and counter was just enough space for a couple of chairs in the corner and room for two or three people to stand. The counter top was glass over timber and under the glass were maps. Lots of maps.

"Akuna National Park is vast." Kane ran his finger from one map to another. "There's so much we still haven't discovered out there. Lots of hidden spots. And keeping those areas pristine matters a lot to me."

"So, what do you do? What is an adventure guide?"

"Everything from taking groups white water rafting to teaching abseiling. Lots of walking tours, some going for several days. One night camping trips for those who just want a taste of the outdoors. Birdwatching tours. If it is doable, I can make it happen." He reached for a brochure from a pile on the far end of the counter and handed it to Nellie. "I've added as much as I can."

You certainly have.

Like his business card, the brochure was black with white writing and way too much of it. There was one photograph—of Kane standing beside his 4WD.

Nellie gazed at the far wall. "*That* is a great photo."

"The river?"

Taken from the middle of a wide river, the photograph was alive with movement and excitement. The water was churning with white tips and ahead, an inflatable raft with half a dozen life jacketed rafters onboard slanted down a small waterfall. They were in a gorge with high cliffs on either side.

"Yes. It would be perfect for the brochure. On the front so anyone picking it up knows immediately they are in for excitement."

Kane leaned his hip against the counter and folded his arms, eyes serious. "You've got my attention. What else?"

Concepts flooded Nellie's brain and she helped herself to a notepad and pen and began sketching. "Front page with an amazing image in full colour plus the business name and contact details. And a cool tagline. Do you have one?" She glanced up.

"Tagline?"

"Short descriptor. Um...have boat, will float."

They both rolled their eyes at that.

"I'll try one," Kane said. "Excitement on the go."

"Experience excitement on the go...wait. A perfect danger awaits. Nah, we can brainstorm one later." Nellie tore that page off and put to one side. "Then we have a bullet point page which is basically a list of what you offer. You can add something about custom tours available on request. This is also the only page without an image but we add the business name again—well a logo. On every page actually, with the phone number."

That page joined the first.

"Now for the fun part. Pick a couple of reviews and match them up with photographs that are relevant. Example, a glowing review about overnight camping with an image of tents beneath the stars. But just a couple. What?"

With a frown, Kane shook his head. "Reviews?"

Nellie straightened. "Off your website or even better, social media."

"Ah. About that..."

He pursed his lips as if not sure what to say.

"You do have social media?"

"Well, yes. Sure. Blair made me set up a couple of different ones last year but I don't have time to add stuff that often. I guess I should."

Nellie tapped on her phone until she found the business on Facebook. "Do you know you have about a hundred followers? And quite a few reviews. This kind is good...Kane Maxwell was a knowledgeable and confident guide and very patient with our questions about the National Park. Five stars."

"Really? Someone wrote that?"

"Here you go. Scroll down to read more and if you don't mind pointing me toward the restroom?" Nellie handed her phone over.

"There's a door off the kitchen." Kane was engrossed in reading, his elbows now on the counter as he scrolled through her phone.

For just a second it occurred to Nellie she shouldn't be leaving her phone with anyone—not with the information she kept on it. But she knew she could trust Kane. How she knew wasn't clear. Yet she did. As long as her feelings of trust didn't run away with her, or develop into something else. Attraction was one thing. Romance quite another.

Chapter Eleven

Kane wasn't a fan of social media but he'd dropped the ball when it came to monitoring the business's pages. There were so many nice comments from people kind enough to leave a review, but also unanswered questions from other people interested in booking with him.

So many missed opportunities.

He needed to hire someone to help with all this. Seeing Nellie so bright-eyed as she'd sketched out the pages of her version of his brochure was inspiring. She clearly knew her stuff and actually got a kick out of doing it. Probably no different from when he was out in the National Park. That was his happy place and one he understood far better than social media posts and websites. They simply didn't interest him.

Somebody tapped on the front door which he'd left locked. He'd moved to the other side of the counter and reached for the lock before looking at the visitor.

Should have ducked behind the counter.

Caryn Corday barely waited for the lock to turn before pushing the door open. "So, you *are* still alive."

Kane wasted no time returning behind the counter. He wanted to keep a barrier between them. "Did you receive the refund?"

With a dramatic eye roll, the woman plonked a huge handbag on the counter and leaned forward. "I told you, pet, I don't want a refund."

She wore a bright pink singlet style top which was pulled down at the front to show the top of a black bra. Kane wasn't one to judge how other people presented themselves but every time he'd met this woman, she'd worn less. Exactly what did she think she was here for?

"Our company policy recently changed so unfortunately, there are no more solo guided tours available."

"You can make an exception, though," she said. "We have some unfinished business."

She reached across and tried to take his hand and as he pulled it away, Nellie emerged from the back. Her eyes flicked from Caryn to his then a small smile crossed her lips and she came to stand close to him. Without a word, she took her phone and slid it into a pocket then brightly smiled at the woman over the counter.

Caryn didn't even look at Nellie. "We need to continue our plans in private, pet."

"We don't have any plans. As we've discussed via text message, I have refunded the full amount of the camping trip which was washed out by the storm. And as I've just mentioned again, we're no longer taking bookings for solo trips."

"Why?"

Good grief. You are why.

"It takes me away from larger groups who need expert care."

"*I* need expert care," Caryn virtually purred before

seeming to remember they weren't alone. "Why can't your hired help manage those groups?"

Caryn looked Nellie up and down with a sneer on her face.

Her condescension was intolerable. Nobody was going to treat Nellie that way.

"You're wrong, Caryn. Nellie isn't my hired help. She's—"

"I'm Kane's girlfriend."

Kane blinked as Nellie slid her arm around his waist but it only took a second to wrap his around her shoulders. Her body was warm and...well, it fitted against his.

For once, Caryn seemed incapable of words. Then she swept her handbag off the counter. "I'm not someone you want as an enemy so I'd reconsider your so-called company policy!"

The woman flounced out, the door shutting after her with a satisfying click.

Silence settled for a moment or two. Nellie made no move to distance herself.

"Girlfriend, huh?" It sounded kind of nice on his tongue.

"Seemed the right thing to say."

"It was perfect."

Kane could have sworn Nellie squeezed his waist slightly before stepping away. Caryn stood on the side of the road, glaring back at the shop. She probably couldn't see inside from there but there was something sinister about her demeanour. It was unpleasant knowing the woman was unhappy. And worrying. He'd never had a dissatisfied customer—although this was obviously something other than a normal response to a cancelled booking.

"Do you think she'll leave a bad review?" he asked.

"No." Nellie gazed at him. "I don't know the backstory

but I can read people pretty well and she has a thing for you."

"A thing?"

"Likes you. Or...wants you."

"Geez. It isn't reciprocal."

"Of course not. I can't imagine you falling for someone so in-your-face and she's far too old for you."

Kane burst out laughing.

Nellie wasn't offended. "Nothing against having an older partner, but Kane, she's a cougar. Or thinks she is. My goodness, if she'd met some of the real deal in advertising circles, she'd..."

Suddenly, Nellie dropped her head.

Don't stop talking to me now.

"Blair wanted to make a bet that you have an advertising background."

She kind of laughed. But she still didn't look at him.

"I don't bet, but you certainly have a great eye for what works. You never told me why you dropped by."

"Oh, yes. There was a reason," Nellie said. She pulled a couple of brochures from her handbag. "I was hoping to get an unbiased opinion. Do you mind taking a look at these and giving me your first impressions?"

What she slid along the counter was a whole world of difference from his pathetic attempts. Both caught his eye immediately thanks to the colour combinations and easy-to-read layouts.

"I love this one."

"Why?"

"The image of your property is great. And I have no idea how you made the words so clear over it but it is easy to read."

Nellie grinned and at last looked him in the eye. "Awesome. That's the way I'm leaning so now I can perfect it. Thanks."

"So, you do this stuff? Make flyers and brochures and business cards?" He re-read the list. "And design logos. What about manage social media accounts?"

A little frown creased her brow. "Never considered offering that. Maybe. I mean, I know how to but hadn't thought of including it." Then she smiled. "If you ever decide you need to update yours, I'm happy to do so. No charge. Give me a chance to make something look good and get results before I offer it to anyone else."

"I think I'll be taking you up on that. I'm going to take a look at what else I've let go and then, can we have a chat?"

"Sure thing. Now, I'm going to discover the rest of the kingdom and leave you to return to serenading whatever it was you were pummelling." She picked up the brochures and slipped one of his among them. "You'd better lock the door again. In case you-know-who sees me leave and returns to try her luck."

Nellie's grin was so cheeky as she headed for the front door that Kane found himself smiling. He'd smiled a lot lately. And the difference in Nellie was nice now that she seemed less worried.

"I think I will do exactly that. Might even lock the shed as well."

Once she was outside, she turned and looked up at him. "Thanks for your help with my brochure."

"Thanks for being my girlfriend."

"Yes, well I never expected to be like in those books where people pretend to be together but it felt right."

"Nellie, I'd—" His mobile rang.

"See you."

94

She was heading off before he could finish his sentence.

Nellie, I'd like to cook you dinner again soon. But for two only.

He pulled the phone from his pocket and glared at the offending device. "Bad timing."

Chapter Twelve

Gigi's Emporium was a curious shop and Nellie didn't know quite what to make of it.

The interior was dim with the exception of a narrow fridge filled with glass bottles of different shapes and sizes. With no sign of other customers or staff, Nellie was drawn to the light. Inside the fridge, some bottles were tall and thin while others were short and round. There were labels which looked handmade and were hard to read. A shelf at the top was filled with jars containing strange mixtures of vegetables...perhaps. Nothing looked appetising and Nellie moved across to a tall bookcase.

One shelf was dedicated to bibles. Nellie counted at least twenty-five and no two were the same. A sign declared *FREE if you replace it with another*.

All around the shop were pieces of furniture and all second hand. Not antiques or restored but old and mainly a bit on the awful side. Lamps with faded shades. Kitchen chairs in need of sanding and repainting. Paintings and hat racks. There was a coat stand which reminded Nellie of the floorboards in her house.

"Came from the old Parson place."

How did you sneak up on me?

The woman at her side only came up to Nellie's shoulder and stared at her through oversized glasses. She must have been eighty but stood straight. Her hair was styled into a bob and dyed blue and green and silver which matched a long dress in swirling patterns.

"But you'd know that already."

"I don't understand," Nellie said.

"You live there."

Okay, this is creepy.

"No need for that look of alarm. I leave the psychic readings to Edwina Lette, but she'd probably tell you there's a ghost living in your house."

"I've already heard that story. Apparently, it scares away anyone who lives there."

The old woman scoffed. "The high rent is what scared them away. That and living so far from modern conveniences. So, when are *you* leaving?"

There was no way to tell if the woman was joking.

"Are you Gigi?"

"See, you have powers of your own." Gigi pointed at the coat stand. "One hundred dollars."

"I'm not buying furniture just yet. But I hoped you might know some of the history of the house. Someone called Parson build it?"

"If you're not buying, then I'm sitting down."

With that, Gigi reached for a walking stick which Nellie hadn't noticed, and limped her way behind a small desk. There was an open bottle similar to those in the fridge and when Gigi poured some into a glass, the liquid was a sickly shade of brown. The woman sipped it and made a smacking sound of appreciation with her lips.

Things couldn't get much stranger.

"Old man Parson fancied himself as a land baron. Arrived out of nowhere one day with the deeds to what is now your land and young Kane Maxwell's place. Kept to himself which was just as well." Gigi leaned back in her seat, which creaked alarmingly. "Not the most pleasant fellow. He built your place for himself and his wife. The other to sell. But nobody wanted to buy. Too expensive and too far. No amenities back then. Water came from a bore and a tank. No power. And the road was dreadful."

"How long ago was this?"

"Must be about forty years now. He had a sweet woman for a wife. Tiny thing with a gentle smile. Never said much. And one day she just upped and left."

Okay, things just got stranger.

"Where to?"

"Nobody knows. In fact, Parson was investigated once the police got wind of her disappearing but it all was dropped when he died."

"In my house?" Why she'd blurted it out like that, Nellie had no idea. She didn't believe in the supernatural.

Gigi cackled and then coughed. She drank the rest of the concoction then took off her glasses and wiped her eyes with a tissue. "Your house is free of skeletons. He ran his car off the road going to Armidale one night. Turns out he had a son in England who wanted no part of the properties and left them in the hands of the agent in Tamworth. Not even with our local folk." Her face screwed up in disgust as she replaced her glasses. "And nobody gave them another thought until Kane decided to buy one."

"Except there have been residents. Even recently."

"Last ones left a few months ago. The agent refused to

repair the steps and they stopped paying rent. Nobody since then."

Then they'd left behind the bed and base. But who had been inside eating takeaway a day or so before she arrived if not a removalist or similar?

"You gonna buy that coat stand?"

"May I take a photo?"

"You young people taking photos of everything. Go ahead."

A couple of minutes later—after politely refusing the offer of a bottle of whatever was in the fridge—Nellie stepped outside. The heat was accompanied by growing humidity and she was thirsty despite the water at Kane's. The next stop was a tiny convenience store she'd not even noticed when she had driven by.

It was an old house with the front room converted to a retail space. Behind the counter, a doorway led to the lounge room so presumably, whoever ran the shop lived behind it. Grateful to find bottled water in the fridge, Nellie took one, then treated herself to a chocolate bar. A girl of about ten took her cash without a word, gazing at her through curious eyes. It must be school holidays still.

Back outside, Nellie found a shaded spot against the building and opened the bottle. At least now she had a place to buy emergency supplies without travelling all the way to Bindarra Creek. Although small, the shop was well stocked with packaged goods as well as having a display freezer with a selection of products.

Nellie headed back toward her car, opening the chocolate bar on the way. Passing Gigi's, she noticed two surveillance cameras outside and had to chuckle after Gigi's disdain of how young people photographed everything.

Kane's yard was locked up and his 4WD gone.

A few cars went by and a truck, all slowing at the lower speed limit from just the other side of the bridge to about half a kilometre past the park. And in the park, a rider on it, a motorcycle idled near her car.

She flattened herself against a tree trunk, sick in the stomach. She pushed the uneaten chocolate bar into the handbag.

It's the same one. Same person.

"No, no, no, no, no." Barely able to draw breath, her words were whispers of despair.

He might not have seen her. His helmet was on but he didn't appear to be looking her way. So why park so close to her car when there was plenty of space?

If only Kane was still at his shop.

But how would she explain herself?

There's a motorcycle that I've seen twice and now I'm terrified?

Besides, he had his own problems with that peculiar woman...Caryn.

This was her problem.

The minutes ticked by and perspiration trickled down Nellie's spine. A low grumble of thunder in the distance had her glancing at the sky. Dark clouds were approaching and at some point, she'd need to get to her car and go home.

Perhaps it caught the attention of the motorcyclist for he also looked at the incoming storm clouds. After a long look in her direction but with no sign he saw her, he was leaving the park, waiting for a moment for a car to pass, before turning onto the road in the direction of Bindarra Creek. Nellie waited until he was out of sight then sprinted to her car. She locked herself in and started the motor, praying he didn't turn back.

Slow, heavy raindrops fell as Nellie dashed to the front door. She'd stopped half a dozen times on the way home, one eye on the clock in the dashboard as it counted five minutes a time and one on the rear vision mirror. If the motorcycle was following, he was out of sight. If it was someone sent by Andre, then they hadn't seen her turn off the main road.

Or else they know where you live and are making it clear they can find you.

Slamming the door, Nellie turned every lock then ran from room to room checking each door and window. By the time she'd finished, the rain was beating on the roof and her heart was pounding.

Back at the front of the house she stood by the bedroom window which was the best vantage to see down the driveway. The rain was intense and narrow streams formed in the dirt, bubbling, and bumping against each other on their downhill race. A white cockatoo flew under the verandah, shaking water from its feathers before settling on the arm of an old chair Nellie had dragged out there. It noticed her and tilted its head.

"I'm glad you found shelter."

So have you, Nellie. Open your eyes to how safe you are.

The road was too far to see but there was no movement outside other than from the effects of the storm. The trees and bushes sagged beneath the onslaught. Lightning hit something close by and with a click, the power went off.

Nellie glanced at the light above her but it didn't come back on.

"Fine then." She went to the kitchen and took candles from a cupboard. Although she had two lanterns, the candles were scented and would help her relax when night fell. She checked the pantry for food. She could make something cold. Except almost everything needed an ingredient from the fridge and she was reluctant to open it. The longer it stayed closed the better and if the power wasn't on in the morning, she'd start cooking everything she had in the hope she could make it last a bit. Even if she had to drive somewhere to buy ice.

Her computer and power bank were charged and she should check her phone. She reached for it in her handbag, instead, getting a handful of melted chocolate. She turned the handbag upside-down and shook it until everything was on the kitchen table. And just about everything was covered with gooey chocolate.

"I really wanted to eat that."

She licked the tip of one of her fingers and screwed up her nose. Terrible idea. There was lint from the inside of the bag, too small to see but obvious on her tongue. Under cold running water, the once delicious chocolate bar swirled around the sink then went down the drain.

"Goodbye, chocolate."

After turning off the tap, she dried her hands and collected some paper towel and the spray bottle of white vinegar she used for most surface cleaning. It was incredible where she found evidence of contact with the chocolate bar. Her purse had some in its zip, the phone had a line of it beneath the protective cover, and her favourite pen needed dismantling to get the last bits out. The brochures were disgusting—apart from Kane's which was sandwiched between hers. And the inside of the handbag still smelled of cocoa after two cleans.

"New recipe, vinegar and chocolate...yum. Not."

Leaving the handbag inside out to air, Nellie changed

into less sweaty shorts and top after a very quick cold shower. She combed her hair, leaving it damp, then slid the chain she always wore over her head.

Her fingers wrapped around the pendant.

This was what Andre wanted. At least, the secrets contained within it.

I'm so tired of this all. So tired of being afraid.

But would handing it over finish this? Should she phone him and arrange to meet him somewhere public? Give him the USB in exchange for a promise not to act on what it contained and to leave her in peace.

She laughed shortly. He'd say anything to get it back.

Nellie opened the front door and stepped out. The storm was passing and the rain easing. The air was fresher and the scent of the wet ground and gum trees filled her senses. What she had to do was bullet proof herself. There had to be a way to do so because she had to make this new life work. The scare in Glenmeer didn't make her want to leave. Over at Kane's house, there were lights on and the hum of a generator. He had the right idea. So self-sufficient and prepared for anything.

And look at me. Reactive and afraid.

How far she'd come since leaving behind her old life. Distance was one thing. But the difference in her confidence and outlook on life had changed, and not for the better.

Chapter Thirteen

The power was still off as evening fell. Nellie's phone was down as well so she couldn't occupy herself with anything internet-based. She'd left the front door open with the screen locked and the same with the back door and the house was lovely and cool from a breeze blowing through. Although the storm was long gone, rain still pattered on the roof but with decreasing velocity.

The sound of a vehicle approaching was the last thing she expected and her immediate response was to panic, quickly replaced by the hope it might be someone from the power company.

It was Kane's 4WD.

She unlocked the screen door and pushed it open as he ran up the steps.

"No generator?" he asked.

"Didn't know it was a thing until I heard yours."

His face fell. "I'm so sorry. I never thought it would carry over the distance—"

"It doesn't. I mean, it does but only if I stand here."

Nellie led the way to the corner of the verandah. "Oh. I can't hear it at all now."

"Only have it on periodically to keep the fridge and freezer going. Do you have much in yours?"

"A bit. Well, a few meals worth. And my only bottle of wine."

Kane laughed. "That is a tragedy all on its own. I guessed you'd be in darkness over here because when the power goes out, it really goes. Last time it was two days."

"Oh dear. You wouldn't have a big esky or something I could borrow? And tell me where I can buy ice?" The thought of all that food going to waste was upsetting.

"Yes. But I also have a large fridge and freezer which are working. How about we empty the contents of your fridge into mine until we get electricity back? There's a ton of space and we can pack yours into containers which you can come and grab as you need."

You've thought of everything.

A week ago, she'd have refused. Made an excuse. But a week ago she'd not spent time with Kane and Blair and the others, let alone overheard Kane singing 'like nobody's listening'.

"Why are you smiling like that?"

"Like what?"

"Like, I dunno...you were thinking of something amusing."

She headed to the front door. "If you're certain it isn't an imposition..."

"I even brought containers with me."

Nellie stopped at the door. "Thank you."

He ran down to the 4WD. "How many do you think?" Kane pulled a heavy plastic container out. It was the size of a baking tray with a lid. "I have about twenty."

"Five? Maybe?"

I can carry the wine.

Nellie was smiling again. She'd never had a neighbour like Kane.

I've never met a man like Kane.

Back up at the top of the steps, he hesitated. "Would you like to take them in?"

He'd only ever been in the house when he'd carried the printer in and that was just inside the front door. Every other time she'd kept him outside, protecting her privacy and safety. Well, now she didn't need those barriers. She stepped aside.

"Please go in. I don't think I could see over all of those."

Somehow, he managed to kick off his boots and push them to one side, then he headed straight for the kitchen. Nellie had forgotten he'd know the layout. There'd been comments about him considering this house before deciding on the one next door. So, what exactly was wrong with this place?

"Kane, why didn't you buy this house?"

"Huh?" He was looking for a place to put the containers.

Nellie rushed to the table, pushing aside the handbag and its contents which she'd still not reconciled. "Whoops. Had a catastrophe earlier with a chocolate bar."

After putting down the containers, Kane gave her a smile. "It melted in your handbag? Better than in a pocket."

"Oh, has that happened to you?"

"Twice. Didn't learn the first time."

For some reason, bonding over melted chocolate was fun. For the next few minutes, Nellie handed the contents of the fridge to Kane and he packed, sorting as he went and it was eye opening. Nellie considered she was a fair cook and good meal planner but he was next level.

"Cooking cream, mushrooms, fresh pasta—have you ever made your own?—cherry tomatoes, basil, garlic, free-range eggs, parmesan. At least two, actually, three meals there. Next."

The wine was the last to come out of the fridge and for a moment, Nellie thought Kane would add it to one of the containers. But he closed them all, one by one.

"I made something nice earlier. Before the power outage. Homemade gnocchi using my own potatoes," he said.

Her tummy was rumbling.

"Plus, some bread which just needs cooking. Garlic and herbs."

"Sounds good. Meanwhile, I'll keep my bread and a slice of cheese."

Kane stopped what he was doing and gave her a serious look. "Why do that? I've got more than I can eat."

Nellie stopped what she was doing. What was he saying?

"After you left, I gave a lot of thought to your ideas. You know, about using better images and stuff for my brochures as well as the whole neglected social media thing." Kane rolled his eyes at himself. "Would you be willing to take a proper look at my business and help me fix how I'm representing it?"

Ideas formed before Nellie could stop them. For some reason, *Glenmeer Guided Adventures* was important to her and she was more than willing to see what she could do to bring proper branding, and customers, to Kane.

"So, what you are saying is that you will feed me and I will help you?" Why did she sound so serious? She'd meant to be light-hearted and open to negotiation but clearly, she'd worked for Andre for far too long. Before Kane could respond, she grabbed one of the containers. "I'm starving so let's get this party started."

———

While Kane cooked, Nellie asked questions and made notes. She'd brought her laptop to his house and he'd opened his own bottle of wine after putting hers into the fridge. Into the main fridge, that was. His bottle came from a narrow, glass-fronted wine fridge.

"I love local wines. By local, the Hunter Valley is close enough to count and there are some decent boutique wineries closer to Bindarra Creek. Do you prefer dry?" He'd looked at her bottle earlier. "Like your New Zealand white?"

"Got a taste for that winery after a trip there a few years ago. Lovely little courtyard where they serve cheese platters. And dry is my preference."

"Tell me what you think of this one," Kane said. He poured two glasses and then made a toast. "To passing storms."

The best kind.

"In the short time I've been living here there's been two big storms. Is that typical?"

"Varies. The weather's been all over the place for the past year or two which makes predicting the patterns difficult. For that matter, it makes planning for outdoor activities difficult."

Nellie was on Kane's website using an offline mode. "So, you have a contact form set up. Do you get many enquiries through it?"

As he took the bread from the oven, the delectable aroma made Nellie's mouth water.

"Not a lot. Most people either phone me or email the address which is on the brochure," he said.

"If we can do some SEO and get your visibility up...but first let's make a plan to tweak the site...like adding a gallery." Nellie clicked around. When there was no response, she glanced up. Kane looked puzzled. "Oh, search engine optimisation and—"

He topped up her wine. "All another language to me. I guess you mean the website needs work and there are ways to get more people looking at it."

"Exactly. Sorry, I don't mean to rattle all this stuff off."

"You're probably used to working with people who understand it."

"True. Although my expertise is in other areas, I've been around enough website designers and online marketers to find my way around social media and websites."

"And what is your expertise?"

Kane began slicing the bread and Nellie gazed at him. Had she said too much? Or was it time to be more open?

He looked up, straight into her eyes, and smiled.

It did something weird to her. A flip-flop of her heart.

"Only ever tell me what you are comfortable with, An-Nellie."

"Annalise."

Oh, my goodness. Did I really say that?

If anything, Kane's smile widened and he reached out a hand, "Well, it is nice to meet you, Annalise."

Instead of shaking her hand, he squeezed it and warmth generated up her arm, little sparks firing through her nerve endings. Any doubts disappeared and she smiled in return before he released her fingers and returned to slicing bread. As if nothing happened.

Nellie closed the laptop as Kane served dinner.

"There's nothing I can help with?"

"You have. And are. Giving me unbiased feedback about my business is invaluable."

"I haven't even begun," Nellie said. "If you'll allow me to, I'd love to put together some simple concepts. A new logo, if you are okay with it, and then all the branding spreading out from that."

Kane placed a bowl of gnocchi in front of her. "I hope you like it. There's fresh basil and garlic and sun-dried tomatoes with a dash of cream."

From the first bite Nellie was in culinary heaven. The little parcels of potato were like soft clouds and the light sauce had the best balance. And the bread? Warm and crusty and melting in her mouth.

Neither spoke until the gnocchi was gone and they both reached for the same piece of bread at the same moment.

"Sorry—"

"No, please go ahead."

They laughed and sorted out a piece each.

"This meal is restaurant quality, Kane. I can't remember the last time I enjoyed anything as much." Nellie spread butter across the bread. "Are you classically trained?"

"I'm motherly trained. Mum was a chef—went to the Cordon Blu school. She only got to use those skills for special events as there's no fine dining, not at her level, in the area. But when we had a family birthday or Christmas, she'd spend hours in the kitchen and always gave me a space to help her. Not so much Blair. He likes to eat but not cook so much." Kane laughed. "Mum tells him off about not looking after himself better."

"And you grow your own produce."

"Nothing beats home grown."

Nellie learned to cook young as her mother was useless

at anything other than fast-food reheating. But she didn't love it. Perhaps now, away from the convenience of a city filled with restaurants and the potential to grow her own food, she could enjoy it.

"Nellie?"

"Sorry. Miles away."

"I want to pay you for anything you do for the business."

Of course, you do. You are genuine and responsible and decent.

"Well, what if you let me come up with some ideas and see what happens? I'd never charge anyone before having a decent concept they liked. Besides, if I can help you rebrand and it brings you new business, I'd ask you for a review."

"I can't even find the reviews on my own page," Kane said.

She giggled. She couldn't help herself. Kane was the first man around her age she'd met who didn't do social media. It was refreshing. And kind of cute.

He raised his eyebrows. "If you're going to laugh at me, I'll withhold the wine."

"Don't do that. I'm not laughing at you," she said. "If anything, your lack of interest in social media is nice. Instead of being surrounded by people who spend every second on their phone, it's a welcome change to have a conversation."

"Good answer."

To prove his approval, Kane poured the remainder of the wine into her glass. There was barely a trickle. "That's a bit sad."

"Would you like to share?"

"What, get two straws? Pretty sure there isn't enough

for a mouthful even. Are you planning on driving anywhere tonight?" He got to his feet and picked up both their plates.

"Furthest I'm going is on foot back to my house."

"Or, you could sleep here tonight. There's a guest room always made up. It has its own bathroom and a lock." He put the plates in the sink then went to the wine fridge. "Better than sleeping in a house with no power." Taking out another bottle of wine, he held it up with a questioning look. "I promise you I would never intrude on your privacy."

It was still raining. Walking back to her house, whether Kane accompanied her again or not, didn't appeal. And he'd already shared a bottle of wine with her so him driving was out of the question. She'd had enough of her house without power.

"Better open that bottle then."

Chapter Fourteen

Despite a late night and another glass of wine, Kane was up before dawn. He'd laid awake for a while after Nellie had gone to her bedroom, listening to be sure...of what he wasn't certain. That she was safe? Comfortable? Having her in his home was nothing like Blair being here. His brother was noisy and self-sufficient and perfectly capable of looking after himself.

So was Nellie. Kane reminded himself of how she'd moved into a house with no power and a roof full of holes and within a couple of weeks turned it into a minor fortress.

And that was the thing niggling at him in the early hours.

She was capable and resourceful. But she was also afraid of something. This was more than just a rural area. It was a safe haven. Living outside the only local town along a narrow dirt road meant few sightseers if any. And nobody breaking into houses. None he'd ever heard of close by. But fear still flashed into her eyes every so often.

Like when I asked about her expertise.

Nellie had withdrawn for a few seconds. And after turning the conversation a different direction had told him her full name. Annalise. A name she'd not wanted to share until then.

He made coffee and went through the back door to sit on a bench he'd made a few years ago. He loved using his hands to create, whether in timber or the garden. This was a nice spot to sit in summer. Warm air and birdsong and surrounded by the pleasant scent of the herbs growing only a few feet away.

"Good morning."

Kane hadn't heard Nellie get up or walk out...her feet were bare and her hands nestled a steaming cup.

"Couldn't resist the aroma of fresh coffee."

She settled beside him, drawing her legs up to sit cross-legged. He'd encouraged her to borrow any of the clothes and sleepwear in the cupboard—left by his mother for unexpected visits—and she'd selected lightweight track-suit pants and a T-shirt with bold writing that 'love is love'. He couldn't help smiling and sipped some coffee to hide it.

"That room is lovely, Kane. You have lucky visitors."

"So, you slept okay?"

"Best sleep in ages. Might have been helped by the wine. And food!"

The sky lightened as they sat in a friendly silence, drinking their coffee and breathing the fresh morning air. A couple of magpies flew down and started their long day of searching for food, digging around in the dirt between the pavers in the entertainment area.

"Most people I know are terrified of them. Always afraid of being swooped." Nellie carefully adjusted her legs so as not to startle the birds. "I always enjoyed having them around and found if I talked to them, they never bothered me."

"Mutual respect works with birds."

"Agree. From my apartment I used to see cyclists being swooped along the path."

Apartment. Another little snippet of your life.

Kane laughed. "Do not tell Blair, but when we were kids, we lived in Bindarra Creek and there was a magpie which took exception to him. No idea why because he'd never harm anything, but he'd ride his bike along the river and get swooped by this one magpie. Year in, year out."

"Poor Blair. I wonder if being near the water makes them cranky? My place in Manly overlooked the water and..."

Nellie trailed off and when Kane looked at her, she was biting her bottom lip.

"Nah. It is just territorial. Some people suggest feeding them but that can mess with their health so it goes back to mutual respect. And talking to them."

Her lips flicked up for a second.

"Are you seeing a lot of birds at your place?" he asked.

"Yesterday in the storm a sulphur-crested cockatoo flew onto the verandah. He or she made themselves comfortable on my seat and gave me a few strange looks through the window."

It was nice sitting here talking. Nowhere to be in a hurry. No clients today.

Once they'd finished their coffees and the conversation had stalled, he stood. "I'm going to make some breakfast. Hungry?"

Nellie followed him inside. "Actually, I am. But you can't keep feeding me."

"Why not? I like cooking for my friends and family."

She put her cup on the table and gave him a small smile. "Does your generosity extend to me having a hot shower?"

"Take as long as you need. I'm making waffles, if you are okay with that?"

"At this rate I may never leave!"

Although the smile remained on her face, her eyes changed. She'd spoken without thinking and whether she was regretting the banter or just unsure how Kane would take it, Nellie was second-guessing herself.

"I'll work out an Airbnb price. Go shower."

Best to be cool about it and not let her see his real response to her comment. He busied himself in the cupboard until he heard the shower turn on, then gazed at where she'd stood a couple of minutes earlier.

You can stay as long as you want.

The shower had been off for a while and Kane figured it was safe to start cooking. He'd sliced strawberries and had butter and maple syrup on the table as well. Before he could turn on the stove, the sound of a car coming up the driveway stopped him.

He didn't recognise the car but he wished he'd stayed inside when Caryn climbed out of it. What in heaven's name was she doing here?

She gazed around then noticed him and smiled. "There you are. I was thinking I'd been misled about your address and made the mistake of knocking on the door over there." She pointed toward Nellie's house. "Well, this *is* nice, isn't it? Plenty of privacy. I like privacy."

"Why are you here?"

Caryn came to the bottom of the steps and looked up. "To see you, of course. Why else?"

"We concluded our business yesterday."

"Business? I hope that's not what you think we have?"

Kane shifted his weight to widen his stance and crossed his arms. Behind him, soft footsteps approached along the hallway. What must Nellie think of him with this ridiculous situation?

"Caryn, how did you find my home?"

"Oh, I spoke to quite a few people in Glenmeer, and you have to remember my mother lives in Bindarra Creek so it wasn't hard to find out. And I found something else out," she said, putting a foot onto the bottom step. "You don't have a girlfriend." Another step. "I am puzzled why you'd make up such a thing. *Kane*."

The way she said his name was nauseating.

"Please leave—"

"Honey? I thought you were bringing me breakfast in bed?"

Nellie pushed the screen door open and joined Kane, sliding an arm around him to tug at his crossed arms. When he dropped them, she held one of his hands. She was wrapped in a towel, her pendant was around her neck, and nothing else.

Caryn's expression was priceless. She stepped back, down a step, almost tripping over her own feet. Confusion was replaced by fury.

"Oh hello. What are *you* doing here? My boyfriend and I are having a special...very special day together," Nellie said. "And I'm hungry. If you know what I *mean*."

When Nellie rested her head against his shoulder, Kane almost burst into laughter. Not at Nellie, who was wonderful, but Caryn's red face.

"I was told on good authority you are not in a relationship." The woman hissed.

Nellie squeezed Kane's hand and kept talking. "You might need to check your source. Besides, this is new. New and special. So maybe the local gossips missed the memo. But I am curious...Caryn. What exactly do you want from my boyfriend?"

The silence dragged.

Caryn clearly was in some state of shock.

"Honey? Should we call someone?"

Probably.

"No, sweetie, I think Caryn was misinformed and now that she knows the facts, won't be dropping by again. Am I right?" Kane directed his words to Caryn.

Whether she understood was anyone's guess as she hurried to her car, dropping her keys twice before throwing herself inside. But instead of starting the motor, she climbed out again holding a phone and before Kane could react, she'd taken a photograph of them both.

"No, no, no..." Nellie recoiled.

Kane was down the steps in seconds. "Delete that. You have no right—"

The woman was in her car before he could reach her, the door locking as he grabbed the handle. He tapped on the window. "Delete the photograph, Caryn!"

She sneered at him as she started the motor.

"Open the window!"

He didn't have a chance. The car was moving now, tyres spinning at first in the dirt, flinging mud everywhere. It got traction and fish-tailed its way down the driveway.

Nellie stood where he'd left her, hand over her mouth and eyes wide.

Kane ran up the steps.

"Are you okay?"

"She took my photograph." Nellie's voice was muffled behind her hand. "Why would she do that?"

"Because she's unhinged. I've gone over and over in my head how she could possibly think I was interested in her. There's nothing. No flirting. Nothing even close. Oh, Nellie, I'm so sorry you've been exposed to this."

Without a word, Nellie ran inside.

"Nellie?"

Kane closed and locked the screen door and followed. Nellie was in the guest bedroom, door shut. He waited in the hallway for a moment then decided that was creepy and went to the kitchen. Fresh coffee might not fix anything but making some kept him busy for a couple of minutes.

"Kane..."

Nellie was just inside the doorway. She'd put on her clothes from yesterday and carried the ones she'd worn earlier.

"I'll wash these and return them. Once the power's on. As long as it comes on in the next few hours. Otherwise, I can't wash them..."

Her face was white and when Kane got close, he was alarmed at how much she was trembling.

He gently extricated the clothes from her hands and put them on a side counter.

"Come and sit and have some more coffee. Caryn isn't coming back in a hurry."

"No. I mean, I can't. I have to pack things."

"I don't understand."

She drew in a long, deep breath and wrapped her arms around herself, not meeting his eyes. "Thanks for last night. For dinner. Everything. I have to get going."

"Get going? That sounds final as you're saying goodbye. Nellie?"

With a brief shake of her head, she'd spun around and was on her way to the front door. Her laptop bag was in the guest bedroom and Kane collected it as he followed her. She was too upset to have remembered it.

Nellie stood at the screen door, one palm on it as she peered through.

Why are you so afraid, sweetheart?

"I've got your laptop bag," Kane said.

She nodded but didn't move.

"Shall I walk home with you?"

"What if she's waiting down the road? What if she's sitting in her car sending that photograph to people? Or putting it all over social media?"

"Nellie. Nellie, can you look at me?" He forced his voice to be calm. When she finally gazed up at him, it was through eyes full of unshed tears and his throat constricted. Ever so gently he touched her hand on the screen door and she turned it to let him envelope her fingers with his. "Why does it matter if other people see your photograph?"

Her lips quivered as she tried to form words. They didn't come.

"You know you can trust me, right? I'm good with secrets," Kane said.

"But my secrets might get me killed." A single tear slid down her cheek. "And if they find me and think you know anything...Kane, I've put you in terrible danger." With a whimper, Nellie flung herself against him and burst into tears.

Chapter Fifteen

The tears were spent. Poor Kane's top ended up with wet patches from them but he hadn't complained or stopped her from bawling against his chest. He'd lifted her into his arms and she'd found herself on his lap on the sofa. With his arms around her and his encouragement to cry as much as she needed, Nellie had let go of weeks of worry. She wasn't one to show her feelings like this. Not by herself and definitely not around other people.

Nellie had finally run out of emotion and sat up. How could she have done this? How could she break down in front of him and cried all over him?

But Kane was gentle with her and had suggested she freshen up and he'd make them some coffee. They were in the kitchen now.

"Coffee for you. Sit tight and drink it and I'll be two secs and make us some breakfast."

If only she'd stayed in the house. Kane was more than able to send that woman packing. But she'd sensed he was unused to dealing with unwanted advances and in her career, she'd come across many people who thrived on using their charms for advancement. She abhorred it. And her presence should have been the end of it but now her image was on someone's phone and she had no way of controlling what happened to it.

That's the point. You can't control what she does, only how you deal with it.

Running away again was the last thing she wanted to do. She was already loving her property. And the town. And...her eyes drifted across the table. There were strawberries and maple syrup and butter. What was that saying about food being the way to a man's heart? Probably worked just as well on women.

"You need to drink the coffee in order to enjoy it."

Kane wore a different top.

"I'm sorry you had to change."

"And I'm sorry that woman distressed you. Up for some food now?"

She nodded and took a sip of coffee. Kane gave her an odd look through narrowed eyes but whatever he was thinking he kept to himself. He lit on the gas burners on the stove and heated a cast iron waffle iron.

"Do you take it camping?"

"Sure do. Client's love taking turns using it even if they've never touched one. Most people wouldn't think of cooking waffles over a campfire but they are tasty."

Kane cooked and Nellie finished her coffee. Her heartbeat was back under control and the trembling had stopped but she was drained and longed to climb into bed and sleep. Once he'd got a small pile done, Kane refilled her cup without asking and pushed the plate toward her.

"Help yourself. There's plenty."

She managed one. It was delicious but her stomach

kept churning and it seemed risky to eat too much. Kane noticed but let her sit quietly as he ate his fill.

Her fingers kept returning to the pendant.

"Nellie, anyone who knows me will tell you I keep to myself a lot. And I don't get caught up in gossip and rumours and the like because it isn't my place to ask questions about someone else's business." Kane pushed his plate away and turned in his chair so that he faced her. His face was serious and little lines creased the corners of his eyes. Not laughter lines though. Worry lines.

Did I put those there?

"And I've not intruded, have I? Not once have I asked about your background or your past. Unlike Blair and Miranda, who were trying to guess about your job, I've left it all for you to talk about, if and when you want."

He was so earnest, so direct. He must have been curious about this strange woman buying a derelict house and then not even coming to say hello. It wasn't a lack of interest on his part but good manners. Good enough to let her cry all over his chest.

"I'm a graphic designer from Sydney. I've lived there all my life and owned an apartment in Manly for years. Had a sports car. Worked for a top-end, boutique advertising firm. Travelled all over the world. And speak three languages." The words came out in a rush.

This sudden download of information seemed to puzzle Kane. He played with his coffee cup, watching her the whole time.

"And Kane, I'm not normally so secretive. But I have good reasons to be."

"And those reasons have something to do with that pendant?"

She dropped her hand and he scooped it up. His skin

was warm and his touch reassured her. How on earth had she let down her guard so fast? How did this man get under her skin so easily?

"You said before that your secrets were dangerous. And might put me in danger," he said.

"And you deserve to know enough so you can protect yourself." It made sense. If he understood the risks, then he could keep himself safe.

But he shook his head and almost growled. "No. This isn't about *me*, Nellie. I've known since the first time I saw you there was fear in your heart. Why else would you hide behind a tree when a car passed your house?"

"Oh. You saw me?"

"I did. And there are the security screens all over your house. The way you clamp up the minute you think you're giving something away. I know you have said you are good at reading people but part of what makes me good at my job is the same—from the beginning I've believed you are looking over your shoulder the whole time."

Those stupid tears were threatening again and only the grip of Kane's hand kept her from crumbling into a heap.

"Ask anything," she whispered. "I'll answer your questions."

At Nellie's request they were seated on the front verandah. She needed to see further than the walls of Kane's house. See if anyone was approaching. And it was illogical and unsettling but her perception was off-kilter.

"Until a few months ago I worked for an advertising agency...I mentioned that earlier. The owner is a man named Andre Canning and even though I've known him for several years, even travelling overseas to meet clients and attend conferences with him, his true nature only recently surfaced." She took a sip of water from a glass she'd brought outside. Her lips were so dry. And her throat was as well.

Kane had moved his chair so he could face her and watch the front of the property. He was clearly humouring her but either way, it gave her a sense of security which encouraged her to continue.

"Andre is competitive. And greedy. If he wants something he'll go after it with almost single-minded determination and he hates losing. What he wants most in the world right now is to buy the business of one of his enemies...a talent agency."

"As in—actors?"

"Yes. And more. The thing is that there are a couple of high-profile artists attached exclusively to that agency which would make Andre a lot of money as their only agent. All the other ads agencies who want them will need to come to him, which ties in well with his need to be the centre of attention."

"Charming character. And the agency isn't for sale."

"Exactly. He tried a direct approach and was knocked back. Then he got a third party to try for a higher price and that failed. The company doesn't have shareholders so he is limited in what he can do and the funny thing? Because he wants it so much, he has to be careful not to damage its reputation or any other tactic which might otherwise make a business owner consider a sale."

She smiled at that. He'd raged about how his hands were tied more than once.

"And you worked closely with him?"

The smile faded. Kane's eyes gave nothing away but it was as if he needed to know.

"The first few years, no. I was just one of the graphic designers. Over time my work was noticed and advertisers asked for me and I moved upstairs to be part of more important campaigns. The ones Andre oversaw. He's talented but a point came when he no longer wanted to do the work. Just the wheeling and dealing. But yes, I did work closely with him and I think he trusted me. He must have, otherwise he'd have never let me see what I did."

Her stomach was churning again and she curled her fingers into fists then noticed, and clasped them together. Otherwise, she'd start playing with the pendant and that would only draw more unwanted questions.

Kane's generator—which had become a background noise Nellie almost forgot about—suddenly stopped.

He got to his feet. "Power must be back." As he walked past her, he touched her shoulder, his fingers leaving heat behind. He stepped into the house. "It is."

Nellie was straight onto her feet. "I'll grab those clothes and wash them—"

"Nellie, stop." Kane held the door open for her but again, touched her shoulder.

He was so gentle that she forced her feet to a halt and waited.

"I thought you'd got past wanting to pack up and leave Glenmeer. Have you?"

I want to stay. Oh, sweet heaven I want to.

"We can't always do what makes us...happy." Why did her voice catch?

"Why not? Look, I may sound like a dreamer but being

happy is central to everything. Family, friends, enjoying one's own company. Doing good because it feels good." He took her hands in his. "Not wealth or prestige. And definitely not fear."

He believed his words. And gazing into his warm, brown eyes, Nellie wanted to believe them as well. If only she didn't have this mess hanging over her head.

"This is a safe place. A safe community. Out here, where the birds are tame and the roos hop around as if they own the place, nothing and nobody—short of a run-in with a wombat—will hurt you." He gripped her hands more tightly. "*I* won't let anything happen to you."

She was wavering. Her resolve to get as far away from Glenmeer as fast as she could had re-emerged the minute the power went on but if there was a chance...

"Besides," Kane tried to laugh but it fell short. "I can't fix my business cards or logo without you." He shook his head. "Scratch that. It sounded manipulative and it wasn't what I meant at all."

Nellie stepped closer until the heat radiating off his body enveloped her. That urge was back and this time she knew she wasn't going to resist it. "Then what did you mean?"

His head lifted, looking anywhere but at her. Then he released her hands and put his arms around her. When his eyes met hers, they burned with a fire which scorched into her soul.

"What I mean is I don't want you to go, An-Nellie. You have to do what's best for you, but I couldn't forgive myself if I didn't say that."

"I don't want to leave," she whispered. "But I don't know how to stay."

With a groan, he tightened his arms until she was

finally hard against his body. "There's nothing we can't face together. Let me help work it out with you."

Their lips were almost touching. And for once, there was no need to answer. He'd said it perfectly. She raised her chin and found his mouth.

Chapter Sixteen

There'd been no more talk of Nellie's past for the rest of the morning.

That one kiss had changed everything. Nellie was happier, more confident. Kane caught her looking over at her house with a worried expression but a touch of his hand to her cheek and she'd released a sigh and turned her back to it.

Back in the kitchen, he heated up the remaining waffles and this time she ate properly.

"Nice morning tea," she said, reaching for the final one with a questioning look.

"Help yourself. I ate more than enough earlier."

After washing up, they loaded the containers of her food into the 4WD and drove to her house. Her fridge was back on and cooling fast and while she unpacked, he fixed a fuse which the power had blown for the lights.

"It was the ghost," Nellie said. She had the sink full of soapy water and was washing out the containers.

"That old story. Where did you hear it?"

"Um...Keith? He cleaned out my water tank."

"Millsie loves his ghost stories. But they're just stories."

"I know all about this house. And yours," she said and handed Kane a tea towel. "Built by an unfriendly man named Parson four decades or more ago. Had a nice wife who disappeared."

Kane laughed. "You've met Gigi." He started drying the containers and putting them onto the table. "Did she tell you his wife was never located and lead you to believe she's buried somewhere in the National Park?"

"I was more concerned she was buried under the floorboards!"

"Nah. You can get under the houses pretty easily and there's only hard dirt there. But it was a pity both homes were left to run down. Mine was lived in a bit more than yours and there were long-term tenants who looked after it pretty well. Even so, Blair and I spent months redoing the floorboards, verandah, and outside decking."

Last container washed, Nellie dried her hands and watched Kane.

"Do you miss him? Blair?"

Kane thought of several answers which fit but went with the most honest one. "Yes. I miss him. But not all of his habits. He's messy and noisy for a start. And is drawn to whatever is new and shiny. Apart from Miranda. She'd been part of his life for years except he only saw her as a friend."

"And now they're together. Well, apart but together."

There weren't any other reasons to stay here. Kane had been trying to come up with something that didn't make him seem like he was just hanging around. He piled all the containers up.

"I'm going to get out of your hair, Nellie."

Her eyes flashed that doubt which he'd hoped was gone for good.

"You okay on your own?"

"I am. Are you okay on your own?"

Now, you're teasing me. Good for you.

He was tempted to say he wasn't.

"Sadly, I have a group to take out later today. Family of four going camping for the first time so there's a bit to prepare...mainly to run through what to expect with them."

Her shoulders dropped.

"Back around lunchtime tomorrow so would you like to have a picnic?" He picked up the containers and started walking toward the front door. "Have you been into the National Park yet?"

Nellie scooted past and opened the door. "No, but I want to."

He took the containers to the car and handed them to Nellie while he opened the boot. "Thanks. Well, now that you have hiking boots, what about a half-hour walk from the back of my property? The climb is steep in spots but there's a decent lookout to reward you."

She glanced up at the hill behind their houses. It didn't look particularly challenging from here because the trees gave the impression of a gentler rise.

"I'd like that. And I'll make the picnic."

He closed the boot. There was still some uncertainty in her eyes but she smiled and it was all he could do not to kiss her again. "Sounds wonderful. Do you want to meet me at my house about twelve? I'll text if I'm delayed. Actually, I can't. I don't have your phone number."

"Well, I have yours. I'll send you a message."

"Don't forget to. Otherwise, how will I phone if I want to ask you out on a date?"

"So hard living so far apart. Go on, I've got a client who

won't be happy if I don't provide some samples soon...don't give me that look, I'm talking about you."

"I knew that," he said.

"Ah, huh."

"Lots of samples, thank you."

"Lots and lots."

He stepped away "On that note, I'm going to work."

Nellie ran up the stairs. "I'll see you tomorrow. Don't get eaten by a wombat."

"They don't eat people."

But she just waved and then was gone, closing, and locking the door behind herself.

While he waited for the family to arrive at the shed, Kane phoned Blair.

He'd gone back and forth questioning himself all afternoon as he'd packed the 4WD for the trip and now that he had nothing to do, dialled before he could change his mind again. Nellie wouldn't want him interfering and he probably should keep his brother out of it, but Blair's talents— plus his return to Sydney—were too tempting.

"Miss me already?"

Kane grinned and perched on the edge of a table. "Hardly. Settled back in?"

"Even went surfing this morning. What's wrong?"

"Why do you think something's wrong, dude?"

Blair's voice was suspicious. "You don't usually phone me unless it is my birthday."

"Fair enough. I have an odd request—"

"You're an odd person.," Blair said.

"Thanks. It's about Nellie."

At least that got Blair's attention and for a few minutes, Kane outlined what happened to her in Sydney. "I'm going to do some searching but you know your way around the city and social media. If you have time…"

"Always wanted to be a detective. But did you say Andre Canning?"

"Why?"

"Pretty sure his firm has a box at Olympic Stadium. I'm sure I've seen it."

A car drove in past the shop and parked in one of the customer parking bays.

"My clients are here. Blair, just some intel. Please don't approach the man or anyone associated with him."

"Of course. Is Nellie really in danger?"

"I don't think so. But she's afraid."

"You seem to know an awful lot about her."

"Got to go. And thanks."

"Hang on—"

Kane hung up. He wasn't about to answer questions about his newfound knowledge of Nellie. Or anything else about her for that matter. Blair had agreed to do some quiet checking on social media to see if anything odd popped up about this Canning person or his company. It was the best he could do until he was home again and could spend some time researching the man.

"Hello?"

Two teen boys and their parents were out of their car.

"In the shed. Ready for some adventure?"

Chapter Seventeen

The printer hummed as it warmed up and Nellie hummed with it. She'd caught herself singing a couple of times during the afternoon and Kane's words resonated—sing like nobody is listening.

When Kane drove past on his way to Glenmeer, she'd had to rein in whirling thoughts about being alone here. Considering she'd bought the property thinking it was the only one in the area, it made little sense to be concerned about his absence. Only a few weeks ago she'd been out of sorts finding she had a neighbour.

But now you kind of like that neighbour.

To keep herself busy, she'd worked on her ideas for *Glenmeer Guided Adventures*.

Using her creative talents filled her soul as much as stepping into a luxurious bubble bath. With champagne. She'd missed this more than she knew and the hours flew by as she built a mock-up of a website, designed several logos, and began the important job of finding the right words. Kane clearly had an excellent business. His reviews —the same ones he'd only just found—were glowing in their appreciation of the experience he'd provided. And that was the point. She was selling an experience, a feeling, a moment of memory making.

This was why clients had asked for her again and again. This was why Andre promoted her so rapidly and then handed over some of his more important portfolios. Which made her wonder how had he explained her disappearance from the company?

She stopped what she was doing. For that matter, how had he explained her disappearance, full stop? Overnight she'd vanished. None of her work colleagues knew what happened. The contents of her desk were probably in a box somewhere. Unless Andre had thrown them out. There were only a handful of people who knew she was on the run and she'd left the details cloudy on purpose.

Her real estate agent who'd sold her apartment.

A neighbour—a lovely older gentleman who she knew would fret if she just vanished. She'd given him the idea that she'd decided to take a new job overseas after he'd seen her carrying bags from her apartment.

Her mother. This had been tricky. She'd told her some story about wanting to take a year to write a book and hoped it would explain a long absence while avoiding anything which would alarm her.

And Cory.

Nellie smiled. Cory was her first friend when she joined Andre's company. He worked several floors down and they'd met on the elevator and hit it off. Cory was a bit like her—obsessed by his job. But he was the one who'd taken her in.

After taking the sheets of printed paper from the tray, she set them down on the table and sent him a text message.

> Checking in to make sure you are going okay.

Apart from the power company, real estate agent and the like, only Cory and her mother had the post box address in Bindarra Creek and it hit her that in a life of thirty-plus years, she only had two people she trusted enough to share something so important with.

She tossed the phone onto the table and took a few deep breaths. How had she reached this point in her life with so few friends? And no network? Looking back, the people she associated with were almost completely in the advertising industry. Her life in Manly was a blur of moments on the beach—usually after hours during summer or weekends—and breakfast in a couple of cafes. Why hadn't she expanded her world to include the people she regularly met and exchanged pleasantries with?

For the first time she could remember, loneliness tugged at Nellie's core.

Her phone beeped.

> More to the point, doll, how are you? I've been worrying.

She should have stayed in touch.

> Busy, that's all. The house is coming along and I'm starting up a small design business. Just for locals, shops, and so on.

Cory sent some smiley faces.

> Lucky them! All I hear from upstairs is how much you are missed and that heaps of your clients are unhappy. Some left the firm.

"No way."

He'd always managed to pick up whatever gossip was happening around the building. Cory called it his 'hobby' and made sure he frequented the local eatery favoured by the other floors whenever he could. Which was funny because he was great with secrets. Just as well.

She started to type a question about Andre and deleted it. Better not to ask. Not to know.

> Andre is furious.

On the other hand...

> The replacement 'you' is a sweet young woman. She won't last. Andre was seen yelling at her the other day for losing a client.

> > That poor girl. He never raised his voice at me in all those years.

> Because he knew you'd leave. You've got a backbone and don't need anyone.

Nellie grunted. More to the point was that Andre needed her to look after his big clients. Which is exactly what she was doing when she stole the object. Looking after one of them.

She sank onto a chair and rested her head in her hands.

The phone beeped three times in quick succession.

> I've sent some of your mail and a couple of things you left behind to your post office box. Let me know when they arrive.

Have to get ready for a date with Mr
Perfect. He's been away so can't wait to
see him. Kisses.

Kisses back. Have a nice date.

Nellie was certain she'd heard three messages and
exited from the chat with Cory. The other one was from
Kane. There was a gorgeous image attached of a clearing
with three tents, a campfire, and the late afternoon sun
streaming through a canopy of trees. And a message.

Getting ideas for the website. And looking
forward to our picnic.

Her smile was back.

Very pretty spot. And so am I. Enjoy the
evening.

Sleep well.

"You too, Kane," she whispered.

The sky was beautiful overhead.

Nellie sat on a boulder where the stream formed a
waterfall. She'd carefully checked for snakes but the area
was clear of everything other than one of the magpies
who'd followed her.

"There's no food, little fellow. And I don't think I should
encourage you to drink my chardonnay."

She'd filled a glass and brought it out with her after
finishing the work on Kane's business proposal. Seeing the

photo, he'd sent made her want to be outdoors for a bit and the evening was warm and enticing. Dinner was home-made pizza and it was ready to put in the oven once she returned.

For now, she wanted to enjoy her environment.

She'd once read about 'sharing the sky'. That all people were only as far away from each other as their view of the sky above. The sky wasn't completely dark but the stars were bright. Without city lights, it was easy to see the constellations.

I'm close to you, Mum.

Regardless of their differences, she loved her mother. Somehow, she needed to find a way to go and see her soon and she was overdue for a phone call. Perhaps tomorrow.

And Cory. Was he enjoying his date? Over the years she'd seen him try and try again to develop a lasting rela-tionship but the longest was less than a year. He deserved more. Cory had a big heart and his lack of a permanent partner was the reason he poured so much of his time into work. It was better than being hurt.

From near the house, other magpies called and the one with Nellie flew away. Of all the birds, these were first up and last to bed.

The waterfall was a soothing backdrop. Not the powerful rush of waves which had accompanied her sleep and waking life for years, but a gentle reminder that water would always be a special part of her life. Once she worked out how to finish this mess with Andre, she'd go to the sea again. Perhaps not to live, but to visit. Maybe Kane would come with her.

"Annalise Fontaine Sinclair!"

Amused and slightly alarmed at her thoughts running riot, she took another sip of the cool wine. Whatever was going on between Kane and herself needed time to sort itself out. She'd never let her guard down so fast. Never kissed a man she'd only known for a few weeks and had spent hardly any time with.

And never had this sense of security with another person.

Even though she'd originally seen him through a lens of suspicion and alarm, he'd quickly disarmed her defences just by being himself. And the physical connection was a power of its own from the first touch. Which was here, when she'd been at risk of snakebite.

Was that why he was easy to trust?

He'd spoken up at the right moment. Reassured her. And let her lean against him until she'd recovered her composure. All with only one question...had she bought the old house. And after that, other times, so few questions. He'd said earlier today he'd known there was fear in her heart so he was perceptive. And kind.

And so good looking.

Pushing all those thoughts aside, Nellie gazed at the sky again. Sparkling stars in a velvet canopy. Night birds and the whisper of leaves high above as a breeze caught the branches. And the trinkling of the water.

This was her home now. And at last, it was safe and secure.

Chapter Eighteen

It was quite something out here, alone in the darkness with the brilliant stars as company. The wilderness wasn't his thing but when it was part of a package deal, one took the good and bad together. If he had to rough it for a while then he might as well enjoy the view. Which included tents and a campfire in the valley below.

His motorcycle was well hidden in a small cave he'd come across. As long as a bear didn't find it...he almost laughed at himself. Only bears in Australia were koalas and they weren't even a real bear. He'd followed the neighbour's 4WD, disappointed Annalise wasn't in it after seeing her over at the house. Now he was out here, he'd stay and observe the man who lived next door.

He believed in knowing what he was up against and if something was going on between those two, decide if he could use it to his advantage. It wasn't the time yet to confront her.

Andre would be furious to know the sweet little thing who'd stolen from him had also replaced him. That's if anyone could believe Andre's crazed comments that night at the office. After the chase down the stairwell proved fruitless, they'd got their hands on security footage and he'd thought Andre would burst into tears.

"Why would she? Annalise...why do this to me? We had so much together."

It was a stupid emotional reaction and didn't speed up the process. By the time Andre stopped ranting and raving, she was out of the building and before they had a chance to confront her, out of her apartment. Though Andre leaving threatening messages on her phone probably sent her running.

With no such emotional attachments, his job was to find her and to recover the USB. He'd done the first easily enough. But he had one shot to do the second and that took planning. Observation and planning.

And then he'd find a nice quiet spot out here to finish the job.

His phone lit up with a message.

> Are you standing me up?

> Sudden business trip. Call you when I'm back.

He might have to dig a grave big enough for two.

Chapter Nineteen

Kane woke with a start. He lay still on the camp stretcher, straining his ears for unusual sounds, anything to clue him in to what disturbed his sleep. With a family of clients to look after, he was easily roused but even so...

Footsteps on twigs and dried leaves was enough for him to sit and reach for his boots. These were inside a zip-lock bag—something he encouraged his clients to do as well to prevent unwanted visitors creeping in. He slid them on and picked up a torch. In a second, he was out of the tent.

All was quiet.

The sky was lightening as dawn approached but it was too dark to see far without a torch. Kane left it off for now as he stood listening.

Forming a circle around the now-extinguished campfire were the three tents. His, one for the parents, and another for the two teens. A little further away he'd set up a portable shower beside a latrine and there was a bin with a lid which was split internally into rubbish and recycling.

Take nothing but photographs and memories. Leave nothing but footprints.

Another crack of twigs breaking. Kane followed the sound.

Often some curious creature...possums, foxes, even the odd deer, would rustle around in a camping area looking for tasty morsels but what he'd heard wasn't an animal. Unless it was huge.

The camping spot was a small clearing in a narrow valley between two ridges. There was a track to drive in but it was generally overlooked by regular visitors. They liked to be closer to the river or where the terrain was more challenging—which made this area his first choice for inexperienced campers.

He walked as far as the 4WD before turning on the torch. Nothing was out of the ordinary and there were no other vehicles. After flashing the light around, he headed back.

The latrine entry flap was open and Kane caught sight of someone diving back into the teens' tent. He closed the flap and grinned. Poor kid probably got a fright hearing Kane walk back.

At his own tent, he hesitated. He intended to change from the tracksuit pants and singlet he wore at night when camping into day clothes, then get a start on the campfire and breakfast. But something wasn't right. The earlier sounds hadn't come from the direction of the latrine. He was sure of it. Unless the kid was disoriented and wandered around first.

He slowly turned in a full circle, eyes scanning the top of one ridge then the other. The tree line didn't extend all the way up in places and in one of those, for an instant, there was a glint of light. It was gone before he could blink and he drew in a long breath.

What he wanted to do was climb up and convince himself nobody was up there, watching the camp site.

What he had to do was look after the campers he had here.

If someone was watching the camp, then why? Normally, he'd assume it was other campers, curious about another group. But that was before Nellie. His heart thudded. If there was any chance her old employer could track her down, would she be alright in her house so far from help?

She chose that property because it was isolated. There are security screens that nobody will get past. And she can phone the police.

Even so...he'd text her once it was daylight.

To say good morning.

He drove up his driveway a few minutes before midday and parked out the front. After the picnic, he'd get all the camping gear out and clean it and repack for the next trip. He preferred to do it here at home and let the small patch of grass get the benefit of him using the high-pressure hose with water from one of the tanks.

Nellie sat on the top step dressed in shorts, T-shirt, and hiking boots. A wide-brimmed hat was beside her. She smiled as he came around the car and a little bit of his heart lit up.

Okay, a big bit.

"Good morning again," he said, stopping with one foot on the bottom step. "You look ready for a hike."

"Me and my friend, picnic backpack."

Leaning against the railing was an oversized backpack

which looked brand new. How much trouble had Nellie gone to?

"Would you and your friend mind if I run in and change? I'd love some water as well."

"Backpack and I are early so go right ahead."

He climbed the steps until a couple below the top and leaned forward to kiss Nellie. A quick touch of his lips against hers and all was right in the world again. She put her hand up to touch his cheek and he got lost in her eyes. There was a change. Not a sign of the fear from before.

"I'm sorry I work you earlier," he said.

"I'm not. I had a long list of jobs to do so an early start was perfect."

She accepted his offered hand and stood.

"Like some water before we leave?"

"Probably a good idea," she said.

He hoisted the backpack with his other hand.

At the door, he grinned at Nellie. "I need my hand back."

"There's a price involved."

Every time he was with Nellie, she surprised him. Under that cool exterior, she was a brightly burning sun.

"And what price is that?"

The smallest flicker of uncertainty crossed her face then she was suddenly on her toes and her lips were close to his.

"One kiss for your hand back." To make her point, she squeezed his fingers rather firmly.

He lifted her hand and kissed it.

"Very funny."

"But I did what you said—"

Then her lips were pressed against his. She dropped his hand, and he dropped the backpack, his arms sliding around her waist to pull her even closer. By the time he lifted his head, he was breathless and a bit incoherent.

"Yeah...um, that was..."

Nellie giggled.

"Oh no," Kane said.

"What?"

"Did you laugh at my kiss?"

"Silly man. Come on, this picnic won't eat itself."

As though nothing had happened, Nellie stepped back and waited for the door to open, only a faint smile giving away her amusement.

Kane had never met anyone like her.

He opened the door and pushed it wide. "Please."

"At least you didn't say ladies first."

She stepped into the cool of the house.

"Hm. There are several ways to reply to that."

He followed her inside, closing and locking the door and then catching up with her in the kitchen, where she had opened a cupboard and was taking out two glasses.

"Be right back."

While he was changing, his phone rang, and it took a minute to unearth it from the pocket of the shorts he'd just added to a hamper. By then the call had gone to voicemail. It was his father's number. While he rarely called during the day, Kane's mother's birthday wasn't far away so he might be formulating plans for the day.

Putting the phone into the shorts he was wearing, he went in search of the glass of water. He'd call his father back soon.

It rang as he entered the kitchen. "Sorry. It's my dad."

Nellie smiled and pushed a full glass of water toward him.

"Hi Dad, can I call you—"

"It's your mother, lad. She's had a fall."

Kane's heart leaped into his throat.

"Ambulance just took her to the hospital and I'm about to follow."

"Fell? But how, Dad? How bad is it?"

With a small gasp, Nellie got to her feet and came to Kane, resting a hand on his free arm.

"Think something broken. She's awake and all that but in a lot of pain. I've got to go and be with her."

The despair in his father's voice shattered Kane.

"I'm on my way. I'll come straight to the hospital, okay? But get someone to drive you, Dad."

"Bye."

"Dad?"

But he was gone.

"Kane?"

"My mother had a fall and is on her way to the hospital in Tamworth...I have to go."

"Of course."

He grabbed his keys and almost ran to the front door. Nellie was right behind him as he closed it after themselves.

"Oh no."

"Oh no, what?"

He pointed at the 4WD which was still packed to the hilt, including on the roof. "I'd rather not leave all of that on the street..."

Kane ran a hand through his hair. Unpacking would take valuable time.

"Well, come on then," Nellie said. She was down the stairs in a second. "You take my car."

He found himself sprinting to catch her as she jogged away. Once he did, they settled into a fast walk. "I can't just take your car, Nellie."

"Why ever not? I know it's not big like yours but it drives okay."

"I'm not comfortable with this." Kane stopped in the middle of the road. "Nellie, I don't know how long I'll be and can't leave you stranded."

"Then I'll drop you there. There's plenty I can do to amuse myself and if you need to stay awhile, I'll come home." She slowed right down and held out her hand. "I'm really fine being your taxi, so will you hurry up, please?"

Nellie dropped Kane at the hospital after making him promise to text the minute he had news. The drive had been quiet as he sank into dark thoughts and let worry wash over himself. His parents meant the world to him and Blair. Mum had always been well. Nothing ever went wrong with her and now in her seventies, she was as trim and almost as active as ever. He'd never come across a couple so in-tune with each other which made the thought of something happening to either...unbearable.

He found his father seated in the main waiting room, leaning on the arm of a chair with his chin in his hand and his eyes miles away.

"Dad?"

"You made it."

"Don't get up, I'll sit. What happened, and how's Mum?" Kane took the next chair. His father's face was etched with concern and exhaustion.

"Silliest thing. We were both in the garden and Mum was hanging up some washing while I cleaned out the cats' outdoor area. They do enjoy sitting in the sun inside their safe enclosure. Anyhow, Mum was asking what I fancied for dinner because she wanted to go and do a bit of shopping. I didn't quite hear what she said as I was scooping out the litter tray and thought she asked what I was doing."

"Did you have your hearing aid on?" Kane asked.

"Don't be cheeky. Where was I? Ah. So, I straightened up, looked her in the eye from halfway across the yard, and said cat poop."

"Hang on. Mum asked what you wanted for dinner and you answered..."

"Cat poop."

Dad's lips quivered. Kane put a supportive hand on his shoulder.

But Dad burst into laughter which he quickly controlled when other people in the waiting room glared at him.

Mum and Dad lived by humour. Kane grew up in a home filled with laughter and good-natured teasing, and it was an ideal environment to raise two boys in. He and Blair continued the trend and it was obvious that his parents hadn't changed in that regard.

"So, your mother was laughing her head off and I finally realised what she'd really asked and began offering recipe ideas such as cat poop pie."

Of course, you did.

The amusement vanished. "She didn't notice where the washing basket was and stepped backwards. Never seen her fall before but she crumbled and was on the ground crying. Her ankle was pretty grim. Weird angle."

"Oh, Dad. Has anyone come to talk to you?"

"Told to sit and stay. And not going anywhere until I know she's okay."

"I'll get us some coffee."

Kane stopped first at the nurses' station. In between answering the phone, the nurse at the desk told him there was no news and someone would be out in due course. He found the hospital canteen and bought two coffees and two sandwiches and returned.

"Don't know about you, Dad, but I was about to head out on a picnic, but this will do for now."

Picnic...where was the backpack?

"Not hungry. I'll take a coffee though," Dad said.

It must still be in the kitchen. Poor Nellie. All that wasted effort.

"Picnic? Is that some new offer with your business?" Dad asked.

"Nah. I've got a new neighbour, believe it or not. She bought the old place and is doing it up."

All of a sudden, he had his father's full attention.

"She."

"Nellie."

"Nice name."

"She's a nice person."

"Must be if you're doing picnics together. First Blair and Miranda and now—"

"Father. That's quite enough."

His dad raised both eyebrows and reached for a sandwich.

Chapter Twenty

"Are you certain you won't stay for a cup of tea or something?"

"Not unless you'd prefer I stay the night, Dad."

"I'm quite sure I can manage and besides, it is high time you two went on your picnic." Kane's father smiled at Nellie from the driveway of his home. "It is a delight to meet you."

"And you, Mr Maxwell."

Nellie stayed in the car while Kane and his father went to the front door. They spoke for a minute or two and hugged, then the older man went inside. When the door closed, Kane dropped his head briefly.

After a moment, he climbed into the car and she handed him a bottle of water.

"Thanks, and I mean, thanks for everything," Kane said. He twisted the lid off and drank half the contents before Nellie had backed out onto the street.

He directed her to the road to Glenmeer and said little else until they'd driven for a while. She cast quick glances his way every so often and caught him with his eyes closed a few times. If he wanted to sleep, then she'd avoid as many bumps on the road as possible. When she slowed to take some long curves, he straightened and finished the water.

"I am so sorry about the picnic. And sorry that the back-pack is sitting in the kitchen."

"The food is all in a cool compartment with ice packs. And anyway, family comes first. I gathered from your conversation with your dad in the car that your mother will be okay?"

Kane nodded. "Broken ankle. Probably torn muscles as well. I got to see her for a few minutes and she was more concerned that Dad would forget to feed the cats or himself than about her injury. The painkillers probably helped."

"I like your father."

"He likes you too. Said once things settle down, I'm to bring you over for dinner."

How sweet he is.

"Now that he's over the scare of seeing her fall, he'll drive himself back and forth to the hospital and once Mum's released, there's plenty of care where they live because it is part of an assisted living community. And while Mum thinks he can't cope without her, he can."

"And you'll check on them?"

He turned to look at her, smiling. "As often as I can."

"You're close to them."

"Yes. Blair, too. They gave us a great childhood."

What does that even feel like?

There was a pit of sadness inside. She generally kept it at bay and hated thinking about what might have been. Or who she might be if she'd had some kind of normal life as a kid.

"I know not everyone was as lucky as me in the parental department," Kane said.

"We get what we get."

"Happy to listen. Anytime."

Nellie forced a small smile. "Some things are best left in the past. How did the camping trip go last night? You mentioned it was a family out for their first overnight stay."

There was a brief silence and Nellie peeked at Kane again. He was frowning.

"Unless you'd rather not talk about work."

"No, no, happy to. I think they enjoyed the whole trip. Easy people to work with, even the teens who sometimes find it all boring. We did a short hike up one of the ridges and they got a chance to take a stack of photos. One of the boys was putting it all onto some social media or other."

"Excellent! Did he tag the business?"

"Tag...oh, okay, I know what that means and I don't know."

"I can see that we need a long chat about all of this, Kane."

"Can you write a list for me to learn?"

"I can. And some cue cards for when you have opportunities."

"Are you joking or being serious? I can't always tell," he asked.

"Half of each. I've got a lot to show you—ideas I've mocked up but they can wait until you are ready. Until you know your mother is doing okay."

He reached a hand out and she briefly held it, taking it back when a curve approached.

"One of the reasons I suggested the picnic was to give you a glimpse of what I see all the time. Gorgeous views over an ancient landscape. There's a feeling...a peacefulness...it isn't anywhere else I've ever been."

His voice had softened.

Every time he spoke about the Akuna National Park,

Kane painted a picture. If he was like this with his clients, then no wonder he had so many glowing reviews. The difficulty was translating the passion and knowledge into marketing materials.

"What if we go on a longer hike? Take me to your favourite places in the park and let me photograph it. And you in it."

"Oh...I don't know about me."

"Part of being in business. But think about it, Kane. I can create a whole gallery on your website of places to visit. Even set up a page of Kane's picks or similar."

"You know your stuff, Nellie."

She didn't answer. For the past few kilometres there'd been a vehicle behind them. A long way behind, just out of her full view but occasionally disappearing as she looked at the rear vision mirror.

A motorcycle.

On the next straight stretch, she slowed.

It caught up a bit and then fell back.

Her heart dropped.

And her eyes kept flicking up to the rear vision mirror.

"What's wrong?"

"Um. Nothing. Probably."

Kane turned to look behind. "The motorbike?"

I'm going to sound paranoid.

"Been behind for a long time."

"Nellie? What else."

"Saw one like it in Glenmeer the day I came to see you. And when I went back to my car, it was parked beside it. Well, idling, with the rider on it."

He still watched through the back window. "Slow down again. Not a lot."

She did and the motorcycle closed in, suddenly going

much faster than before. It loomed behind the car, tailgating, and then zoomed around and was gone in a matter of seconds.

"Caa.rap." She breathed the word out.

"You okay? Pull over if you want."

Nellie shook her head.

"Was that no, you are not okay, or no you—"

"I'm fine, Kane." It sounded sharp. "Sorry. As much as my rational mind tells me I'm invisible out here, the other part—the scared me—jumps at shadows. Or in this case, motorcycles. But it did look like the other one."

"We'll keep watch. If we see it again, we'll look for a rego number and have a quiet word with one of the local police."

About to say that was a terrible idea and the police were the last people she'd talk to, Nellie bit her lip. Kane wouldn't understand her concerns about Andre's influence in high places because he'd never met him. Instead, she nodded at Kane without saying anything.

Evening was closing in as Nellie drove up Kane's driveway. She wanted to retrieve the backpack from the kitchen and with a bit of luck she could salvage some of the contents.

His 4WD loomed in the shadows and as the headlights caught it, Nellie gasped aloud and braked.

"What?" Kane had been tapping on his phone and his head shot up. "What the heck?"

He was out of the car in seconds, and after turning off the motor and putting on the handbrake, Nellie followed, leaving the headlights on.

The doors on the driver's side were spray-painted with a word.

Two-timer

Kane ran around the other side of the vehicle.

"Same here. Dammit, why. Why would anyone do this?"

"Is it damaged? I mean, apart from the paint?" Nellie began to check the tyres and windows and Kane did the same. "Seems okay at least."

She switched off her headlights and returned to Kane. "This is terrible."

"Let's go inside. I'll phone the police."

Nellie hesitated. She couldn't be here when they arrived. But Kane needed her support. She could take off shortly.

"Nellie..."

She sprinted up the stairs behind him, stopping when Kane pointed. The screen door was open and the front door showed damage around the lock and door handle.

"Almost like someone used a small crowbar to leverage it open. Stay here and I'll look inside."

"Not a chance." Nellie grabbed his hand. "Stronger together."

He kissed the top of her head and stepped inside.

Room by room they turned on lights and checked for signs of damage or theft. Up one side of the hallway, then into the kitchen.

"Where's the backpack?" Kane asked.

It wasn't in the kitchen.

The back door was locked and they worked their way forward to the main bedroom.

Kane pushed the door open.

There was no need to turn on the light.

The room was lit up with a dozen candles burning on

the floor around the bed. On the bed, a picnic blanket was laid out and Nellie's lovingly prepared food was set out on two plates. Her brand-new backpack was in two pieces with cuts across both. And on the wall behind the bed was more spray painting.

Cheater

"Oh, Kane."

He led her back into the hallway and pulled out his phone. "I'll find out how long before the police can get here and we'll check your house."

Her house?

Nellie hadn't even considered this might be bigger than one person's vendetta against Kane. Obviously that Caryn person was behind it, unless Kane had other disgruntled rejectees lying around. He spoke for a couple of minutes to someone he obviously knew then after hanging up, came to Nellie and put his arms around her, drawing her close.

"When I asked you out on a picnic, I expected a nice hike, good food, and wonderful company. Not you driving me to my parents and back for a family emergency and then...this. I'm so sorry."

"Not your fault. But you know who did this."

He released her and nodded. "I don't have any local ex-girlfriends and none who would behave this way. The only person I can think of is Caryn. Let's go check your place out."

"When are the police arriving?"

"At least an hour."

Thank goodness.

"Unless my house..."

158

Kane looked grim. "Hopefully not. Hopefully she doesn't know where you live and is just lashing out at me."

Nothing was touched outside or inside Nellie's house.

Between the two of them they thoroughly checked the house twice and then walked around the verandah as well as the grounds closest to the home.

"I'd say she doesn't know. If it is Caryn, I'd be the focus of her anger, I think."

Kane glanced at his watch. "We'd better go back. Have you met Abby Taylor?"

"Is she the local police?"

"One of them. She's a tough cookie but as nice a person you'd ever meet and incorruptible."

They were at the top of the steps. Nellie had all the lights on. She'd double checked every window and the door was locked, apart from the front door. The sky was almost completely dark.

Kane was staring at her. "Are you coming?"

"Um. Actually..."

"You don't have to but knowing Abby, she'll swing by to introduce herself and ask for your take on what you saw at my place."

And then what will I do?

"Okay, no, of course I'll come back." She quickly closed and locked the front door, pocketing the keys. "I'm not thinking."

Before she could run down the steps, Kane put his hands on her shoulders. "Are you stressing about meeting Abby? She's nice."

"No. Um, I'm sure she is."

Her eyes couldn't meet his and she felt rather than heard him sigh.

"Nellie...she's one of the good guys. At some point, you'll need to stop being a hermit."

"I know. And I'll try."

His finger was under her chin and he gently lifted it. His face was close to her face. Those warm eyes of his searched hers and she could have lost herself in their depths. The worry and fears evaporated as she leaned in and then his lips were on hers and the whole world was spinning in the best kind of way.

Chapter Twenty-One

Who knew kissing was so good for calming the soul?

This thing...whatever it was...with Nellie, was burning into his heart. It wasn't just attraction. She was special.

She'd had such a haunted expression that he hadn't been able to stop himself from comforting her and that led to falling into her gorgeous eyes and then he had no hope. Nellie drew him to her in a way no woman ever had done.

Back at his house, they figured the kitchen was the safest place to be. Apart from picking up the backpack, there was no indication the intruder had handled anything. Even so, Kane found a pair of silicon gloves and wore them as he made coffee. Nellie was pacing, stopping periodically to stare out of the window, arms wrapped around herself. He still hadn't decided if it was because of the damage to his car or a concern about meeting the local police.

Which is puzzling.

Why would Nellie avoid the police? Was it because she'd stolen something? Her motives were pure. Surely, she wouldn't be in trouble for doing the right thing?

"Someone's here." Nellie stopped stalking around the kitchen, her eyes wide.

"Hello? Kane, it's Abby."

"Good hearing." Kane smiled at Nellie.

He'd propped the front door open but hadn't heard the paddy wagon drive up. Nellie didn't follow him as he went to greet Senior Constable Abby Taylor, who'd gone back down the steps and was inspecting the 4WD.

"Hey."

"So, my question is who did you upset?" Abby grinned but her eyes were sharp.

"I think I know the answer."

Abby got him to hold her torch so she could take photographs of the graffiti. "House?"

"Front door forced open and damage in the bedroom."

Before she could go up the stairs, Kane returned the torch. "Just so you know, my new neighbour is inside. She's a bit nervous about meeting new people. Nellie went out of her way today. Mum is in hospital and—"

"Oh no, I'm so sorry. How is she doing?"

"Broken ankle and she'll be okay in time."

"Please pass on my best to her and your father. We do miss them both."

Me too.

"I will. Anyway, Dad rang earlier to tell me about the accident and the work car was loaded up from last night's trip. Nellie drove me to Tamworth, rather than waste time unpacking my 4WD and when we returned, this was all a bit of a shock."

"And Nellie bought the other Parson place?"

"She did. Doing it up and starting to build a small business."

Abby gave him a serious look. "And why is she nervous about meeting me?"

"Anyone, really. She's quiet. Moved here for a tree change from Sydney and likes to keep to herself."

"But drove you to Tamworth."

He had to admit Abby missed little. She was a good person and an excellent police officer. But his allegiance was with Nellie right now.

"And a good neighbour."

Abby did a visual check of the damage to the front door. "Small crow bar, or maybe a car jack. Let's take a look at the bedroom," Abby said. "You mentioned you know who is behind the damage?"

They made their way inside where Nellie stood in the hallway, hands clasped behind her back and a small smile on her lips. But her whole body looked stressed, as if she was ready to run for her life. After her eyes flicked to his for a second, she stepped forward and extended her hand to Abby.

"I'm Nellie Sinclair. Nice to meet you."

"You too, Nellie. Abby. Must have been quite a shock finding Kane's vehicle like that?"

"It gets worse." Nellie gestured to the open bedroom door and Abby went in.

"Oh boy, you're not wrong."

Abby spent a few minutes taking more photographs then joined them in the hallway. "We'll dust for prints but not until first thing in the morning. You'll need to stay somewhere else tonight, Kane. I'll snuff out the candles for you to prevent a fire."

"We are pretty sure we know who did this so is that necessary?"

"It is. I've seen something like this before—not in

person but photos." She took out a notepad. "Tell me your theory."

For the next few minutes Abby took notes while Kane, and occasionally Nellie, recounted the strange behaviour of Caryn Corday.

"She claims that her mother lives in Bindarra Creek? Any further information on who that might be?"

Kane shook his head. "Last thing I wanted was to ask any personal questions. But I do have her credit card details and car rego from the original booking." He hesitated, unsure whether to mention the photograph until Nellie caught his eye and nodded. "The other thing is that Caryn took a photograph of Nellie, who was wearing just a towel—"

"Actually, I had shorts and a bra on underneath but even so..."

"Oh."

"I just wanted her to believe I had nothing on."

"Oh."

Abby grinned and closed the notepad. "I'll go snuff out those candles. Tell me what you need from the bedroom and I'll grab it for you."

Kane raised both eyebrows as Nellie, who was clearly amused at his lack of ability to say anything other than 'oh'. She waggled her own eyebrows back at him. Nellie was a shining light in all of this.

Abby walked out with Kane and Nellie. "I'll message you once we've investigated and will do my best to get you back inside by tomorrow afternoon."

Kane, trailed by Nellie, followed Abby back to the 4WD.

He'd switch on the spotlights along the front verandah and under their stark glare the words on the sides were even uglier.

"What happens next? And what if she comes back?" he asked.

"Doubtful she'll return. She's got something out of her system by vandalising your property. I'm going to run some checks and see what comes up." She gazed around. "Geez, nobody would cross into this light!" Abby opened the door of the paddy wagon and climbed in, winding the window down as she pulled the door shut. "Call us if you have any concerns. At least you're not going too far. Happy to drop you both over there?"

"Walking will help burn off the irritation," Kane said. "See you in the morning."

Much as he wanted to stay in his house tonight, Kane had little choice other than to accept an offer from Nellie to stay in her guest room. They followed the vehicle down the driveway, Nellie holding a torch and Kane carrying his laptop and a small bag with a change of clothes. Neither spoke until they reached her front door.

"You sure it's okay for me to stay? I can grab a tent out of the 4WD and—"

"I'm happy to have the company, all things considered. Now, let me cook for you for a change."

Kane and Nellie ate a delicious meal in her kitchen. Nellie said it was her one good dish, a creamy mushroom pasta. He would happily have eaten it twice over.

"You cook really well," he said, topping up their wine glasses. "My mother would enjoy this. Despite her early

French training—or perhaps because of it, she always preferred simple ingredients done well."

"I like simple. When I was juggling school and stuff, if I wanted to eat it was easier to have a dozen or so meals which were quick used common ingredients and then rotate them. My mother often complained but she wasn't the one cooking."

"Sorry...you did all the cooking?"

She shrugged and twirled fettuccine around a fork. "My mother led a rather odd life and I never knew when she'd be home, or gone for days. At least she always left money in a tin in the cupboard so I wasn't about to starve." Nellie slid the forkful into her mouth more elegantly than he could ever hope to eat pasta.

"I am so sorry, Nellie."

Her head tilted in question as she finished her mouthful.

"No kid should have to raise themselves."

After a sip of wine, Nellie went back to twirling the fettuccine. "Plenty of kids worse off than I was. There was a roof over my head and I wasn't ill-treated. But in my final year of high school, I went to live with my father because Mum got too hard to be with. She's not well now. Cancer."

As calmly as she spoke, there was a glint in her eyes which tugged at his heart. He changed the subject to a story about him and Blair playing in a cricket match as teens and how they'd managed to run each other out. "Blair blamed me and all the way to the change room he kept muttering about his unfit older brother. The reality was that I'd called no, but he thought we could outrun the throw of the ball and took off. He was already halfway down the pitch and rather than holding my ground I ran as fast as I could, throwing myself onto my stomach to slide the last few feet with my bat outstretched."

"But not fast enough?"

"Almost. Had I started a couple of seconds earlier I'd have got there. But I'd called no. Anyway, after the match we were given a round of applause by the other team for entertaining them with our stop, start, go back's and 'run faster' yelling at each other."

Kane chuckled. Blair was unpredictable back then but talented. And he knew it.

"Do you still play?" Nellie pushed her plate away.

"Cricket? Only the occasional social game. Over summer I'm pretty busy with the business as well as being a volunteer fire fighter."

She leaned forward, eyes wide. "You are? Isn't that dangerous?"

"There are risks, but protecting the National Park is something I'm passionate about and a lot of training and practice happens in our team. Quite a few landowners in and around Glenmeer are volunteers. I'll show you around our station one day."

"I'd like that." She got to her feet and collected both plates. "Cricket sounds safer."

"Not when Blair's playing."

———

Once the table was cleared, Nellie left Kane to pour the last of the wine and went to get the work she'd been doing for him...what she called her 'concepts'.

"There's a few...oops, can you grab this top lot?"

Kane caught a couple of folders as they slid out of her arms. She managed to keep the rest contained and joined him at the table. "I'll just sort these a bit. There are five concepts and for each one I've printed a brochure, mocked up webpage, business card slash fridge magnet, shop signage and er, car signage."

Their eyes met.

"You do have insurance for the car?"

"Sure do."

"Good. If you have to have work done on it to remove the graffiti, then you might be able to use some of the insurance money to update the logo on the doors. But that's a discussion to have with the sign writer and insurance company once the police have done their job."

Once she'd made five neat piles, Nellie sat.

"Last of the bottle, I'm afraid." Kane handed her one of the glasses.

She flashed him a wry smile. "Time to order some more. I'll need to find a bottle shop which stocks from that winery. Now, please have a look with an open mind. Everything is changeable and I'm only using my ideas and need your thoughts to continue working on them." With that, she picked her glass, pushed her chair back a bit and crossed her legs, her eyes on him.

No pressure.

Whatever resistance he'd had to changing his branding vanished with the first sheet of paper he picked up.

Bold, vibrant colours drew his eyes first, then clever use of reviews from his social media pages. An image—with a watermark—of a gorge with rapids, wasn't from Akuna but even as a place marker sent a shiver up his spine. And that was just the beginning. He worked his way through all the concepts, each one as good as the last.

"This round is about finding colour combos which resonate," Nellie said.

He shuffled the piles back into their order.

"How do I choose? Nellie, I've never seen anything so professional and creative." He picked up a brochure. "*I* want to book a tour!"

"Good. I'm on the right track then. Take them home when you go. Put them around the house or put some up on the fridge with magnets. Take a couple of days to get used to them and see what draws you. I have my thoughts so I'm curious about where we land on this."

For a while they chatted about the different options and Nellie took notes. Already, images were in his mind about places to take original photographs and Kane couldn't wait to take Nellie hiking to see if she agreed with his ideas. First, deal with the vandalism and intrusion and then make some plans. It would do them both good to be out in the fresh air and safety of the National Park.

Chapter Twenty-Two

Nellie tiptoed from her bedroom to the kitchen, not wanting to wake Kane if he'd managed to sleep. She couldn't. Images of Andre and the motorcyclist popped into her mind every time she'd closed her eyes and her thoughts went round in circles. What if her location had been discovered? What if the man on the motorcycle was here to retrieve the USB?

Ridiculous.

Annoyed at herself, she'd climbed out of bed and tossed on a dressing gown. She got a glass of water from the jug in her fridge, the empty shelves reminding her of the lovely ingredients she'd made into the picnic.

And that grated on her nerves on a whole new level.

How dare that woman open her backpack and make a mockery of the picnic Nellie had prepared! She'd taken one look at the plates and shuddered. The lovely French loaf had been hacked into two giant pieces instead of fine slices. Nellie had intended to create little morsels of deliciousness by topping the bread with a selection of cheeses, pickles, and homemade guacamole.

But Caryn cut the beautiful cheese into ugly chunks and turned the dips upside-down on a plate then mixed them all up and stuck crackers into them at odd angles.

Grr. I'd like to—

Before she could work herself up anymore, Nellie returned to her bedroom. She connected her phone to the charger then opened her laptop. Kane had given her administration privileges on his Facebook page and she might as well use her sleeplessness to do something, such as small updates to the security settings.

Cross-legged on the bed, she logged in. His business page was the same as last time she'd looked. He really had no interest in updating it and she thought it best to leave until he decided about his new branding. Then she could upload everything in one go, along with any photographs and little teasers. A couple of ads would work wonders once all of that was in place.

There was a new review which she clicked on.

"No. Oh my gosh..."

There was a photograph. Nellie in the towel with Kane. Her face was clear enough to recognise and the pendant was obvious around her neck.

Her fingers went straight to touch it. There was no reason anyone would suspect how important this was.

Single women beware!! Kane might be handsome and seem nice but he is a predator!! After going out on an overnight camping trip with him I had to insist he drove me back to my car. I could not believe how he came on to me. We were alone miles from nowhere. So terrifying!! Even his girlfriend didn't know about his two-timing.

Nellie made a screenshot and for good measure, unplugged her phone and took several photographs. Then she changed the setting allowing reviews on the page. With no way to delete just one, it was better—in the short run—to hide them all. Hopefully there would be a way to get rid of that review and if not, she'd talk to Kane about starting a new page instead and delete this one.

Before hiding it, she'd opened a new tab with the profile page of the reviewer.

Unbelievable.

Caryn hadn't even hidden that she'd written the review. And she had posted it on her page as well, which obviously had full public settings seeing as Nellie could read everything. She took more screenshots and reported the post. This was tricky. She had no way to stop anyone finding the image and if Andre or anyone close to him saw it, following the trail to Kane would be easy. A glance at the time told her it was too late at night to bother Abby Taylor but in the morning, she'd send the images across to the number on the card Abby had given her earlier.

She took a look around the page.

Only half a dozen friends.

The page was several years old and populated with copied memes, political rants, and screenshots of newspaper reports. Most were about high-profile divorce cases. And one from a couple of years ago about a man who was killed by his wife after she found out he was having an affair. Caryn had made two comments.

"Cheater. Two-timer."

"Oh, you are a smart woman, not." Nellie reached for her phone again. "Gotcha."

"I've already made a claim with the insurance company for the vehicle. Because of how remote I am, they are happy with the photographs rather than sending an assessor, and once they get a copy of the police report, they will make a decision," Kane said. "In the meantime, I have a friend heading over who removes graffiti for a living. He's going to take a crack at it and at least remove the worst of the words."

They sat on the verandah with coffee as the police did their work next door.

"Abby was very nice when I spoke to her earlier," Nellie said. "she said that checking social media was a common device she uses and that I'd saved her some time. Apparently, she's found where Caryn lives and someone will be visiting her very soon. I just hope..." Nellie pressed her lips against each other, unwilling to worry Kane more.

But he somehow could read her thoughts. "You said Caryn only had a few contacts? And she'd only put that post up on my business page a couple of hours before you found it?"

Nellie nodded.

"Odds are nobody saw it. Not the photograph or the text. And even if it was seen, there's no reason to believe Andre would find out." Kane put his coffee mug onto the railing and took one of her hands. "The police should be able to get Caryn's page taken down, or the photo removed, or even just persuade her to do so. I think once she's got the police in her face, she'll back down fast. Things are going the right way."

His hand was warm and comforting. And his logic was good. Glenmeer was a tiny town. Bindarra Creek was small. And both were in the opposite direction Andre would expect Nellie to flee toward.

"I always talked about having a cottage on the North

Coast. Andre had friends in Byron Bay and said I should get a holiday house but I told him he didn't pay me enough to live there. Lovely area but expensive. I'm hoping he thinks that is the general direction I'd go."

"You should talk to Abby."

"What? About him? No."

"She can help."

Nellie sat back, taking her hand with her. Kane frowned and picked up his mug again.

Her stomach filled with butterflies. Ones with teeth which nipped at her insides.

Must you overthink everything?

Kane gazed over the front of his property and his fingers tapped at the side of the mug. His lips were tight against each other in a straight line. With a small sigh, Nellie reached out her hand again and even though he didn't look her way, he took it. And held it firmly until his phone beeped a message.

"Abby. We've got the all clear to return."

He gave Nellie his full attention. "There's no need for you to help."

"Let's go and see. I can make more coffee if nothing else."

The bedroom was worse than before with fingerprint residue on the wardrobe, bedside tables, window sills, and all the plates and cutlery.

"Cleaning the wall seems the least of our worries," Nellie said. "Wonder what else they've dusted."

It wasn't a pleasant sight walking into the kitchen. Residue was on every appliance as well as the sink and several surfaces.

Nellie leaned against Kane as they gazed around. "Any chance you know how to remove this?"

"Nope. But my friend might. In the interim I'll grab a rubbish bag. But Nellie, as I said before you don't need to help. None of this is your problem."

"Would you help me clean up if it was my place?"

"Yes, but—"

She raised herself on her toes to kiss his cheek, effectively silencing him. "Come on then. I'm going to throw everything away in your bedroom...well, the gross mess which was once a picnic."

Before he could protest, she'd helped herself to a large rubbish bag from a cupboard, then took a couple more. "I think I need some of your gloves if you have spares. Can't bear to touch a thing that woman touched."

It was mid-afternoon when Nellie got home. Kane's house was in better shape, thanks to his graffiti-cleaning friend coming to the rescue with a recipe for a spray to remove the fingerprint residue. There was still work to do such as repainting the wall behind Kane's bed, but at least now he had a freshly made bed to sleep in and an otherwise clean room. After they'd run out of ingredients for the spray, Kane decided to go to Tamworth to see his parents and to shop and insisted Nellie go home. His 4WD was no longer declaring him a two-timer but the paintwork would need redoing and he planned to get some quotes while out.

She was restless.

The events of the past day and a poor night's sleep were messing with her emotions and she found herself doom scrolling on social media. She liked the term. *Doom scrolling.* Made it sound like she was on a mission to visit hell or something when the reality was far less exciting. After a few minutes of reading clickbait and laughing at stupid memes, she exited social media and typed Andre's name into the search bar.

There was the usual guff about him. The official profile with his background and achievements. An article high-lighting his recent success with an advertising campaign for a highly sought-after client.

"Which I created and implemented."

There were new images of him out on a yacht with several men she recognised. Each was someone he'd done business with whether advertising or investments. There was probably enough combined wealth on that one fancy boat to keep a small country running for a year. Or a decade.

What were you all plotting?

There was always something going on in the background.

There was a photo he was tagged in despite it not being about him. Nellie clicked on the newspaper article. It was an annual charity event from two nights ago, one she'd been to a few times representing the firm because Andre swore he'd never personally support the organiser—Carlo Bianchi, the owner of the talent agency he so desperately wanted to buy. She would attend and hand over a large cheque and say all the right things. Carlo had always been pleasant to her although he had no respect for her employer. She read the short article which made no mention of Andre then enlarged the image. There were a few familiar faces in the crowd. And there, standing to one side and glowering at Carlo was Andre.

Nellie recoiled at the venom in his face.

"Why...why were you there?"

His eyes were trained on the host and the image was clear enough to see his hands formed fists. Worse though was the fake smile for the camera. A smile which she knew was kept for occasions when he wanted to hide his feelings.

Except I know you too well.

Chapter Twenty-Three

He was at the end of his patience with this nonsense.

The sudden departure of Annalise and her boyfriend had created an opportunity. He'd watched her arrive at the man's house and wait with a backpack. If they were going hiking that gave him a small window of time to get inside her house. But then they both ran back to her place and disappeared off in her car. Clearly some kind of emergency and with a bit of luck, one that would keep them away long enough for him to find a way inside.

He'd only tried one window when a car flew past leaving a trail of dust.

A moment later, a screeching cry had him rolling his eyes. All he'd needed was a few minutes peace and quiet. The screeching turned into semi-coherent screams. *Cheater. Creep. Two-timer.* All repeated over and over. Yet, nobody was home next door.

When the noise stopped, he'd left the verandah and crept across to the fence. The car was parked behind the 4WD which was being spray-painted by a woman.

Holding back a laugh, he'd moved to a better place to watch.

She wore tiny shorts and top, high wedge shoes, and giant sunglasses. All the time she sprayed, she muttered words but too quietly now to identify. Clearly, she was nuts. Calling the police would have been amusing but it didn't hurt to have someone distract Annalise and the bloke for a while.

"Get it out of your system and go," he'd whispered.

No such luck. She stalked up the steps and disappeared into the house.

At this point he'd moved to the back of the property, up past the stream and boulders into the treed area he'd spent so much time in lately. And that's where he'd stayed until the minute the police car arrived. He'd moved further into the park, to a spot where there was enough view of the back of both places to get an idea of activity, as long as he used his binoculars.

Now, the following day, he was ready to pack it in and return to the city, Andre's potential wrath and a pile of money not as important as his sanity. Police back and forth, both homeowners around, no chances to get into her house without being caught. When the police van rocked up and he had clear sight of Annalise on the man's verandah, he'd made a quick run to her house. It was a waste of time. Everything had security mesh—not that he'd be unable to get through it but he'd need the right tools and time. He couldn't help himself though. He moved the pot again. It hadn't bothered her last time but she needed to start seeing she wasn't safe.

Because she wasn't.

Not by a long shot.

Chapter Twenty-Four

Nellie was watering the herbs in the pot near the front steps when the paddy wagon drove up. She'd taken a photograph of the pot two days ago after yet again finding it wasn't where she remembered leaving it. So far it hadn't migrated again and with no other signs of unwanted visitors she'd decided all the stress had messed with her memory.

The patrol car parked and Abby climbed out as Nellie descended the steps.

"Good morning, Nellie."

"How are you?"

"Have some news. Tried to tell Kane but he's not home." Abby leaned against the front of the vehicle with a smile, gazing beyond Nellie at the house. "Making it look lived in again."

"I'm determined to turn it into a welcoming home. Lots to fix and change but I've got plenty of time."

"Kane mentioned you're starting a business. Home renos?"

Nellie couldn't help laughing at that idea. She could handle a paint brush and make a room look pretty with the right furniture and fixtures but that was the extent of her abilities. "Not me. I design things. Logos, business cards, any type of advertising. I'm working with Kane to make over his branding and hope that will get some interest from other local businesses."

"I'm happy to pass on your details to a few people so let me know once you're up and running." Abby gave Nellie her full attention. "Graphic designer? Ads person?"

Always the questions.

"You said you had news. Is it good?"

Although Abby's eyebrows raised for a second with the change of subject, she nodded. "Caryn Corday has a bit of a history. What she did in Kane's bedroom? I recalled seeing something similar come over our communications and it was connected to her. Had a big breakup with her partner a while back after he cheated and she trashed his place, the new woman's place, several cars, and stalked them both. But it was down in Goulburn. Her mother died years ago. She's moved up here and decided Kane was her next boyfriend."

"For goodness sake."

"Once confronted, she spilled her guts. We found the paint canisters, a stack of photos she'd taken, mostly of Kane but some of you, and enough illicit drugs to make her face some serious charges. She's currently in custody being assessed for her mental health."

Nellie's gut twisted. "Photos of me? What kind? Where from?"

"Main street in Glenmeer, there's one of you getting into your car at the park there, and outside Kane's business."

"Does she own a motorcycle?"

Abby looked puzzled. "No. At least, we didn't find one at her property. Why?"

"No reason."

"There's always a reason. Look, I know you don't know me, Nellie, but I'm just trying to help. Why a motorcycle? Have you seen one around which seemed suspicious?"

Only following me and parking beside me.

She mustered a smile. "When Kane and I were coming home from seeing his parents the other day, there was one behind us for a while. When I slowed, it shot past but I just wondered if it was her."

"I'll look into it."

"Are the photos of me printed or online?"

"Printed. Happy to give them to you once we don't need them."

"Thanks. Hate my photo being taken. By the way, Kane's gone to Tamworth. His mother is being released from hospital and he'll take her home."

"That is excellent news. I'll head off then and send him a text later." Abby opened the door but didn't get in. "I'm really happy to see you living here. The place needed some love and our community is very welcoming. Please always reach out if you need anything. Anything."

Nellie waved as Abby drove away.

The relief about Caryn was real. But the image of the motorcyclist haunted her and the knowledge there might be more photos of herself online made her feel ill.

She went back up the steps and stared at the pot. Was it Caryn who'd moved it both times? There was no way Andre knew where she was. And there were hardly going to be other people messing around with her things. It didn't matter now because Caryn wasn't going to be bothering

Kane anymore so it was time to put this chapter behind herself.

Nellie opened the door at Gigi's, her eyes going first to where she'd last seen the coat stand. It was still there.

"Knew you'd want it."

Gigi was behind her small desk with another bottle of the strange drink in her hand as she poured it into a glass filled with ice.

"I bought a hall rug the other day and think this might complement the entry area."

"Two hundred dollars and it's all yours."

"It was one hundred dollars last time." Nellie picked up the coat stand and weaved her way to Gigi. "Not worth a dollar more."

"Antique."

"Doubt it. What does this price tag say?" Nellie turned a small tag tangling from one of the hooks. "Seventy-five dollars. Even better."

"Trying to make an old lady go broke. And there I was thinking you were such a nice person." Gigi grinned and took a long slurp of her concoction.

Nellie took two fifty notes out. "I'm sure I'll be back to buy more from you. But can I ask...I notice you have surveillance cameras outside. Do they work?"

Gigi almost snatched the cash, holding it up to the light then scrunching it to see if it bounced back. "If you're concerned about being recorded while you hand over your money then I'm going to check these are real."

Unable to help herself, Nellie burst into laughter.

"You can laugh. I've had fake notes in here before. Besides, who uses cash these days?

"Me. But I was asking because last time I was here, there was a motorcyclist acting a bit weird. I just wondered if you might have footage I could view."

For a long minute it looked as though Gigi would refuse. Her head shook from side to side and she muttered something about crazy outsiders. But then she opened a drawer in the desk and pulled out a long key.

"Do you know how to use it?"

"A key?"

"The video machine. I don't. But you can go look all you want. I've seen a motorcycle hanging around a lot lately but the rider never comes in. Never takes off their helmet. Just cruises up and down and then leaves. Go through the curtains and then the room is on the left. And lock it when you're done."

Before Gigi could change her mind, Nellie moved the coat stand to where it wouldn't be in the way of other customers and followed the directions. On the other side of the curtains was a small, dark room with only candles for light. There was one armchair and paintings on the walls... morbid images of a devilish afterlife. Nellie found the door and turned the key. It was all quite strange. In here at least there was an overhead light, although only a naked bulb, and a table holding a monitor and top of the line surveillance recorders. She'd seen similar at work in the past, just on a bigger scale.

Pushing aside the question of why a tiny bric-à-brac shop in a drive through hamlet needed such expensive equipment, Nellie set to work. A search on her phone provided answers on how to drive the thing and soon she was looking at surprisingly clear footage from the last time she was here.

Not only did she see the motorcycle, but Caryn taking photographs from across the road, ducked partially down behind her parked car. Nellie captured some video and stills on her phone in case the police needed them.

There was a good shot of the motorcycle slowing to pass her, the rider's head turned to look at her just as she remembered. Pausing the footage, she took another photograph and zoomed in. The licence plate was visible.

The phone beeped a message.

I'm home and have a great idea.

Her heart sped up as she smiled. Kane had spent the last couple of days dealing with the fallout from Caryn's attack and she'd hardly seen or spoken to him.

Tell me more.

There wasn't anything she could do here unless she planned to spend the rest of the day searching for random images.

I will once you're here.

"Okay, I bite."

Be there soon.

After locking up she returned the key to Gigi, refused the offer of one of those drinks again, and lugged the coat rack out. She had to put one of the back seats down to accommodate it but was finally able to close the back door.

All the way home she sang.

Her spirits were high now. She would send Abby the images but first, she'd go to Kane's house and find out what this great idea was.

"No more Caryn. And with you sending those images of the motorcycle to Abby, that is another worry out of the way, right?" Kane poured two glasses of iced water. "I feel happier and you look like there's a weight off your shoulders."

Nellie wasn't quite ready to admit how much the attack on Kane's property had affected her.

"How is your mother? And your dad?"

Kane joined her at the table and handed her a glass. "Both are doing well. Mum's ankle is set and she needs to use a wheelchair for a while rather than crutches. Just until her first check up and the doctor will evaluate it then. You know what's funny? She is annoyed she hasn't met you."

"Me?"

"Apparently Dad went on a bit about how nice you are."

Heat rushed to her face.

Kane chuckled. "But she's on the road to recovery at least. And Dad is managing pretty well."

"I'm happy to hear that. The last thing anyone needs as they age is to run into a health issue."

"Like your own mother?"

She nodded. "But Mum led a hard life. Well, by hard, I mean she didn't care for herself at all and drank and smoked. And now she has lung cancer." It hurt more than she could say. All those wasted years between them. And this new separation. It wasn't fair.

"Nellie?"

Kane was closer than she'd realised and he touched her cheek. His eyes were sympathetic and worried all at once.

"I need to see her."

"Then let's make it happen."

Tears prickled at the back of her eyes.

"How?"

"We could go to her house. I'll drive."

Nellie giggled at the idea of Kane's dusty, kitted up 4WD parking outside her mother's somewhat posh apartment block.

"I mean it. Is this Andre dude likely to have your mother under surveillance? And even if he is, why can't we go in disguise? For a start, he doesn't know me and won't imagine you are with someone, so all you need is to wear a hat or something."

"Actually, he's only ever seen me with my hair much darker and very long. Now I'm natural again he'd have to look twice." Even if it was just to spend an hour with her mother to see for herself how she was...how wonderful. "I might ask my friend Cory to check in on her and report back."

"So, in the meantime, would you be up for a bit of hiking?" Kane sat back.

"Is this the great idea you texted me about?"

"With the issues with Caryn and my 4WD, I postponed the couple of tours I had booked to next week so I'm free of any business obligations. Might be a good time to go take some photos for the website and stuff. As long as you—"

"Yes! I'd love that, Kane." Nellie tapped her feet on the floor in excitement.

"Is overnight okay with you? Thought we could cover more ground that way."

"Perfect. When?"

"Today, if you want. Or early tomorrow."

Nellie gulped down the rest of her water then was on her feet. "I'll be back in an hour. What do I need to bring? And what about food?"

Kane laughed. "Hiking boots. Three sets of underwear and socks in case you get drenched. Waterproof jacket. Change of clothes. Swimwear. Charged phone for when we have coverage."

"And taking photos. I just need to take the coat stand out of my car and then pack and I'll be back."

"One hour."

At the kitchen door, Nellie stopped. "What if I'm late?"

"Go without you."

Kane had the most serious expression on his face but his eyes danced with amusement.

"Stop it," Nellie said with a grin.

"Stop what?"

About to blurt out something about messing with her heart, she clamped her lips tight against each other and shook her head. When he began to head her way, she waggled a finger at him as if telling off a naughty kid and made a quick exit. Before she could make a total fool of herself.

Chapter Twenty-Five

"There's a left turn ahead in about two hundred metres. Pretty hard to see until you're almost on it."

"Good thing you have local knowledge." Nellie peered ahead through the windscreen of her SUV.

"Good thing you didn't mind driving us to the beginning of the track."

Minutes after Nellie had dashed home to pack—in a mood he didn't understand—Kane had a call from the Bindarra Creek spray painter who he'd arranged to repaint the 4WD. They offered to collect the vehicle this afternoon and have it back to him in four days. All things considered, that was the ideal scenario.

The biggest problem was getting to the part of the park where he wanted to hike from which was several kilometres in, up hills and across country.

Nellie hadn't hesitated to offer her SUV for the trip up and even suggested he drive. But he trusted her and besides, it gave her the chance to experience the roads. Her vehicle wasn't fully off-road but would more than able to manage to get where he wanted.

"Here?"

"Good spotting."

Nellie took the turn slowly which was just as well as a huge pothole had developed since his last trip. She went around and cast him a quick glance. "Is it all dirt roads now?"

"Yeah. Keep watching for potholes but otherwise it isn't a bad road."

It was narrow with thick bush on either side. Soon it would wind upwards.

"You're doing well."

She shifted gears. Rare to find an SUV these days which wasn't automatic but Nellie's was pretty old. "How far?"

"Few minutes. Have you always had this?"

Nellie laughed aloud. "This thing? Um, nope. Until recently I had a sports car. Zoomy little number which suited me to a T. Convertible, which let me fit a surfboard. Well, not very legally but still. And cute as."

What else don't I know about you?

Clearly, a lot.

"You surf?" he asked.

"Sure do. Nothing like the wind in my hair as I ride a wave back to the beach. One of life's best experiences."

"That's what Blair says."

She glanced at him again. "He moved to Bondi Beach, didn't he? That's such a different lifestyle from living in the bush."

"He loves some of it. Definitely the beach and that whole thing of the ocean. And he loves his job but not nearly as much as he loves Miranda. I think he'll end up having a little beach shack on the coast and persuading her to go there a few times a year."

Nellie smiled. "Best of both worlds."

"Do you miss it?"

"The city? Not as much as I expected. But the ocean. Oh, yes."

And one day, when Andre is no longer a threat, will you follow your heart and return to the sea?

"Just up ahead the road splits in two. Take the right part of the fork."

After following the road for a few minutes, it ended at a small carpark with a toilet block and little else. They parked in a shady spot and once the camping gear was out of the vehicle, Nellie locked it and zipped her keys into an inside pocket in the backpack Kane had provided. He'd dug one of Blair's out of a cupboard when she'd arrived back at the house with a duffel bag and had made a mental note to replace the new one she'd bought which was ruined by Caryn.

Nellie gazed around. "It is so peaceful."

"Wait until we are further in. Are you good with the backpack?"

She shrugged it on.

"Blair is considerably broader across the shoulders and body. Start tightening from the strap above your hips." He talked her through each step. "Comfortable?"

"Left shoulder isn't right. Can you try?"

Kane adjusted the strap and smoothed the padding. "Better?"

The corners of Nellie's lips quirked up for a moment.

"What?"

"Maybe all the straps need adjusting." She blushed bright red and ducked her head down with a mumbled, "Forget I said that."

As if.

He gently lifted her chin with his fingers and brushed his lips against hers. "One can never be too careful."

At least she was smiling again and her cheeks weren't so inflamed.

As he strapped on his backpack, he ran through that same set of rules he laid down for any client. Watch where you step. Don't go off the main track without checking first. Stop for water as needed. Say if you feel unwell, light-headed, or tired. And so on. Nellie listened and nodded her head every so often. Understanding and adhering to these commonsense guidelines avoided dehydration and unpleasant encounters with anything that bit or stung.

"Has anyone ever ignored all of that?"

"Funny thing." Kane squashed a wide-brimmed hat on. "The only ones I need to watch are those who fancy themselves as wilderness experts. Newbies are great to work with. Ready?"

In a few minutes they'd reached the camping ground he'd last been at and something made him gaze up at the top of the ridge. Nothing flashed or caught his attention but he still wanted to take a look up there another time. Or maybe they'd walk back that way.

"This is where I bring most of the overnight clients. Protected and not too taxing for those unused or unable to climb or manage heavy ground. I have a lovely couple in their eighties who stay here for two days at a time every few months. They wander as far as the closest creek and he'll fish while she reads."

There was no answer and when he glanced at Nellie, her face had the strangest expression. A bit like earlier at his house. Her eyes shone when she finally looked at him. "What a beautiful thing to do."

"Fish and read?"

"Facilitate two older people to do something which must mean a lot to them both. Not everyone cares about the elderly."

It never occurred to him he was doing anything out of the ordinary but on reflection, there was more work involved for him and every step of the camping process had to be slightly adapted to make it user-friendly for them.

"No different though from someone in a wheelchair and before you ask, yes I have clients with special needs."

She reached out her hand for his. For a while they walked in silence, hand in hand. And it was one of the best feelings Kane ever had. This woman at his side surprised him with her compassion and humour and warmth. How on earth had she settled on Glenmeer as the perfect place to live?

Perfect for me.

"Where are we going first?"

He stopped them both as the open camping area changed to dense bushland.

"For the purpose of photographs, there's a gorge about two hours walk from here which is well hidden and quite beautiful with a waterhole which changes from green to blue depending upon the time of day and light level. And if you want to swim, it is the sweetest spot there is."

"Kane."

"Nellie."

She laughed and the sound filled his heart. It was as though the weight of the world was lifting. Her eyes were alight with happiness and even her body appeared more relaxed.

"Kane. Why are we standing here? In two hours, I'll be starving so can we just start this adventure please?"

Hands on her hips and head tilted to one side, Nellie Sinclair was more than his neighbour. More than a friend.

I've fallen in love with you.

The words swirled around in Kane's head as they hiked, echoing in his heart with each step.

While his friends were all married with several having families of their own, and even Blair was settling down, it just wasn't a priority. He'd dated now and then but those ladies had not shared his passion for the outdoors and his remote home. And if he had to dig a bit deeper, he was shy. Not with his family or his clients, but otherwise introverted. His own company—along with time spent with his parents and Blair and a few close friends—was enough. And work and the property kept him busy.

But this quiet and smart woman he walked with had found a way into his heart without trying. She probably didn't even realise, although her small touches and occasional kisses said otherwise. If he could only find the right words to tell her how he felt.

The track narrowed to almost nothing and Kane moved ahead, following a way through the trees and undergrowth he'd memorised over the years. At the base of an incline, they stopped for a drink of water.

"Does anyone else know where this secret place is?" Nellie clipped her water bottle back on her belt and moved her shoulders to relieve the pressure from the backpack.

"Not many. I only came upon it by accident and have yet to see another group there. Best that some areas aren't readily accessible otherwise they run the risk of being spoiled for future generations."

"The environment matters to you."

"Should matter to us all. Not to mention the importance of respecting the traditional landowners. We're fortunate to be granted such freedom to enjoy this region and I hope that is the case for a long time."

Before he had the chance to launch into a full lecture on the subject so dear to his heart, he checked Nellie was good to keep walking and again led the way. There wasn't sufficient space for anything other than single file and it gave him time to clear his head. Nellie wasn't his target audience for these speeches. One of his dreams was to bring small groups from schools to the more untouched areas of Akuna National Park and ignite a sense of wonder and commitment in youngsters to protect the future of the bushland and all it held. Once he'd established his business more, and could hire another couple of guides, then he'd formulate a way to make it happen. And with Nellie's help on the marketing side, Kane truly believed this was possible. Nothing would stop him.

"You've not said a word in ten minutes, Nellie. Should I be concerned?" Kane reached across the picnic blanket where they both sat and brushed a lock of her hair back.

Her eyes, which had barely left the vista before them, flicked to his, wide and almost with a sense of wonder. "How do you not stay here? As in, always?" Her voice was hushed. "I don't want to go."

Kane understood. They were on a flat rock overlooking part of the gorge, shaded by Kurrajong trees, and appreciating a light breeze which tempered the worst of the heat of the early afternoon. Below, a waterhole had formed millennia ago as the river forged a gorge with water once faster and higher than today's meandering and gentle flow. At one end, a waterfall cascaded.

"Where do you do Whitewater rafting? This river doesn't seem full enough or is it seasonal?"

"Another couple of hours walk away. Back toward the carpark then to the Akuna River. Have you ever rafted?"

With a small sigh, she picked up a salad roll he'd prepared earlier, Nellie nodded. "Not for a long time though. I'd love to do one of your rafting trips."

"As my marketing manager or a client?"

She smiled widely. "As a thrill seeker." With that she took a large bite, her eyes drifting back to the scenery.

"Let me see...how about white-water rafting, abseiling, a cave dive, and some rock climbing? I've run a few three-day tours doing all the above and they're not for the faint hearted."

Nellie adjusted herself so she was facing him rather than the gorge and took a minute to finish the mouthful. It was cute the way she clearly needed to answer but was too polite to talk with her mouth full. Kane helped himself to a second roll. He had no issues with eating while admiring the view.

"When can we go?" she asked.

He chuckled.

"No, really. I would love that so hard."

"Pretty tough on the body," Kane said.

She made a spluttering sound. "I surf. Used to surf."

"So, you want to surf down the rapids?"

Nellie pulled off a small piece of bread and threw it at him.

"Okay, okay. I give up. You can book in when I do the next one in about three weeks. Just don't hurt me anymore."

She burst into laughter.

Once they'd both eaten and packed up again, they stood on the edge of the rock. "We can have a swim if you like."

Nellie leaned her head against his shoulder as if it was the most natural thing in the world.

"We won't spoil the water?"

"Considering how many birds and animals use it...I doubt we'll do a thing to harm it. And I would love to cool off, so is that a yes?"

Chapter Twenty-Six

Above her was the bluest sky Nellie had ever seen.

Around her was the coolest, clearest water she'd ever swum in.

She floated, buoyed by such depth beneath her she'd not found the bottom—not in the middle, anyway. And she'd gone looking. For the first time in months her body was fully relaxed and her mind was clear. The ocean always calmed her spirit and now, in this naturally formed fresh-water pool hidden away in dense bushland, the same soothing effects washed over her.

"Worth the hike?" Kane's head bopped up and down as he paddled closer. Droplets of water sparkled on his shoulders. His muscular shoulders.

"Um...hike? Oh, yes, well worth it." She lowered her legs so she was upright in the water, her feet slowly sweeping back and forth to keep her in the same spot. "This is surely one of the wonders of the world."

"Should be."

"Any idea how deep it is?"

"None. And please, no more disappearing beneath the surface for minutes on end."

"Like this?"

Taking a breath, she sank with barely a ripple. The quiet roar of pressure filled her ears and bubbles rose from her nose. She didn't go far, just enough to see Kane still easily above the water. And below it. Every bit of his body was...perfect.

Seriously Nellie?

She kicked and rose back to the air.

"Not funny, Annalise. I have no idea how you do it but I have no hope of staying underwater as long as you do." He splashed some water her way. "You didn't sign my indemnity paperwork so no more diving."

"Or what?"

Nellie backstroked away, kicking up the water more than she needed.

He might have claimed to not hold his breath for long but he made up for it with speed, switching to freestyle and catching her in a matter of seconds. With a grin, he reached for her foot and she ducked into the depths again, coming up behind him and splashing him. But this time he was prepared and Nellie found herself trapped inside his arms.

"Got you, mermaid."

She wiggled—not very convincingly. "There are no freshwater mermaids."

"Are you certain?"

"Have you ever seen one?"

He was paddling them toward the edge of the pool and when they reached it, he slid Nellie onto a rock just beneath the surface so that she was out of the water from the waist up. He seemed to be standing on something and was at the same height. "Well, a mermaid has extraordinary abilities to swim and dive."

"Okay, I'll play. That one's on your list, so, tick."

Kane's hands floated onto her forearms and the touch was electric. Water and electricity made for a powerful response.

"Mermaids sparkle in the sunshine."

"Isn't that vampires?"

He traced his finger around droplets of water on her skin. "These sparkle."

"Fair enough. Tick."

Her words came out a little breathless as Kane turned his attention to her hair, smoothing it back from her face. "And pretty hair. Silver and gold rolled into one."

"I guess I'm a mermaid."

"But I forgot the most important part."

Why does this feel so right?

Kane held her loosely within his arms, his face close to hers. "Mermaids are smart and funny and have kind hearts. And they are very, very beautiful." His lips were almost on hers. One tiny move and they would touch. "Say it, Nellie. Say tick."

"Tick." With a small sigh she moved an inch closer. "Tick, tick, tick."

It was hard to leave the special, hidden place where time had stood still for a while, but Kane wanted to reach a particular spot for photographs before mid-afternoon, so after a few more kisses in the water, they'd dried and dressed and packed up the picnic. As they reached the summit of a ridge, both stopped for a final look, Nellie dropping her head onto Kane's shoulder. She'd never forget this day.

"Next time we'll plan for a full day here. Okay?" He dropped a kiss onto the top of her head. "You got enough photos for now?"

"I'd rather not share them with anyone but you." Nellie straightened and checked the straps of the backpack. "Too perfect to tell the world it exists."

"I know what you mean. Ready?"

Before reaching the first camping ground, Kane veered in a different direction and the ground rose.

"Seeing as we're so close, I want to check a spot from my last trip out, as long as you don't mind?"

"Happy to follow." She caught up. "What's special about it?"

"Well, it's at the top of one of those ridges above the camping ground so there's a decent view up there. It'll give you a chance to photograph the area where my beginners and so on start off."

"I get the feeling there's more to it."

He glanced at her. "You are perceptive. I didn't see anyone but there was some movement around my camp and I thought...probably a trick of the light, but there may have been a torch or campfire up there. It isn't a usual place for campers as its too open and I'm curious."

Were you being watched? But why would anyone watch you?

Nellie's heart thudded heavily. There was no reason to worry. Nothing to indicate Kane was in anyone's sights now that Caryn was out of the picture.

"When were you here?"

"Before Caryn broke into my house, if that's what you're thinking."

"It might have been her."

"Definitely."

The tension drained away. Caryn had been up to no good for a while. The video from Gigi's shop proved that.

The terrain became rocky underfoot and their progress slowed as the incline steepened. As the trees thinned then virtually stopped, the heat from the sun was almost burning. Thank goodness for a wide-brimmed hat and sunscreen.

From here the view was breathtaking. Nellie stopped and shrugged off the backpack and they both drank from their water bottles. They stood on a wide rocky ridge between two valleys. The one with the camping area was narrow and deep while on the other side, the lower landscape went for kilometres and was covered in eucalypts and Kurrajong trees.

"There are caves." Kane pointed. "Can you see there?"

A small gap in the bushland revealed a cliff face and a couple of darkened areas which must be the cave openings.

"How deep are they?"

"They vary. Akuna has a lot of caves and some were used by bushrangers."

"Can we go and see?"

Kane laughed. "As far as I know, those closest ones are little more than shallow formations and no old relics left behind. But yes, they are more or less on the way to the river so if we keep up a good pace we can stop there."

Nellie pulled out her phone. "In that case, you go and look for the evidence you wanted and I'll take photographs."

She couldn't believe the quality of images on her phone but was quickly developing an urgent need to buy a top-of-the-line camera with several lenses. Perhaps even some infra-red for special effects.

"Why do you look so serious, Nellie?"

Kane was back and she hadn't even noticed the time vanish.

"I think I need to buy a camera."

"Is something wrong with the phone? I have mine."

"Not at all. But imagine the beautiful shots if I had a telescopic lens." She put the phone back into her pocket. "How did you go?"

He gestured toward the caves. "Shall we head over? I'd think whoever was up here was going it solo and camping rough. We get that a bit."

"So...not Caryn."

Why did that bother her so much?

Kane laughed shortly. "Can you imagine? She'd be complaining about the open air, the mozzies, nobody to set up a tent for her."

She couldn't let it go, even as they started down the rocky path. "Do you still think you were being watched though?"

"Probably not and you need to stop stressing about it. Caryn is out of the picture so let's enjoy the day." He stepped down off a rock and turned to offer his hand. "Still going okay with the pack on?"

Nellie let him help her down. "No complaints from me."

"Not even about the open air?"

"Especially about that."

The first cave was disappointingly small. There was barely room for both of them at the same time and so they moved along to the next one.

"Might take a break anyway," Kane said, undoing the hip strap of his backpack. "Have some more water. Are you hungry?"

"After that picnic lunch? Nope. But I'm thirsty."

Backpacks on the ground in the shade, water drunk, they peered inside the cave. The entry was high enough for Kane to walk in without ducking but he hesitated and turned on a small torch he'd taken from a side pocket of his pack. He flicked it around and then stepped inside.

"Okay for me to come in?"

No reply.

"Have you been eaten by a dragon?" Nellie called.

"Someone's been in here."

Nellie followed his voice and then his torch. He was a few steps inside a space the size of a small caravan. The narrow beam of light didn't show much of the walls or ceiling because it was trained on the middle of the floor. There were the remains of a fire, recent from a lingering smell of charred timber and partly burned papers. Rubbish was scattered around. Wrappers from a fast-food restaurant, empty drink bottles, and cigarette butts.

"Nellie? Look at the soft dirt over here."

Kane trained the light onto a layer of sandy soil. Imprints of shoes—boots probably—and something else.

"Is that a tyre track?"

Nellie took out her phone and opened the torch app. She peered closer before moving over to where the food wrappings were scrunched up. Her stomach turned. She'd seen wrappers from that fast-food joint before. She turned the light onto the deadened campfire where a scorched notepad was almost completely destroyed. Something made her poke at it with a splinter of burned timber. There was one page in the middle only yellowed by the heat of the fire. On it was a handwritten phone number.

Her new, private phone number.

Her hand shot to grab her pendant and her heart jumped.

"Hate to say it but this looks like a motorcycle tyre track," Kane said.

He was here.

Nellie stumbled to the wall where she doubled over and vomited.

"Hey...sweetheart?"

In an instant Kane was at her side, his hand on her waist as her stomach emptied its contents. He scooped her hair out of the way and made soothing sounds. Much more pleasant sounds than those coming from her gut. When there was nothing left, she straightened with a shudder, her head away from him. Embarrassed.

"Step over here, sweetie. I'll get some water."

He was gone for a minute and she wiped her mouth, hating the bitter taste and loss of control.

"Water. Drink and spit some out. Then drink properly."

He pushed a fresh bottle into her hands and she followed his instructions until her mouth and throat were less disgusting.

"I'm sorry." Her voice was croaky.

"Stop it. I know what you're thinking and I agree. We're going to head out and find a spot where we can make a phone call. Okay?"

Nellie's heart rate came down a bit. Kane wasn't making a big deal over what happened and if anything, he was on the same page.

"We need photos. Those wrappers are from the same place as the ones left in my house."

"Huh?"

"The night I moved in...someone had been in the house. There were wrappers like that on my kitchen table. I thought it was from the previous tenants or something."

Suddenly she was enveloped in Kane's arms and he held her so close that she could barely breathe.

"You are the bravest person I know."

Brave was the last thing she felt. Terrified. Worried. Angry.

Hold the anger. It'll help.

"How dare Andre do this? How dare he send some henchman to follow me?" She pulled back a bit and pointed at the fire. "My phone number is written on the notepad, Kane. Only my mother and you and Cory have it."

"Go outside and put your pack on. I want to record what's in here and take photos and then we're going."

The tone of his voice left no room for debate and Nellie wasted little time strapping the backpack on. Her eyes darted around, expecting someone to come out of the bush to grab her. She checked her phone but there was no coverage here. They need to get much higher up.

And fast.

If the motorcyclist was anywhere nearby, they needed to get to safety.

Chapter Twenty-Seven

Nellie's reaction in the cave had shaken Kane. She was terrified and he'd led her straight to the one place she should never have been.

Except we wouldn't have known if we'd not explored.

Her instincts had been right all along, believing somebody had been around her house and seeing patterns with the motorcyclist.

"I wish you'd said something," he said. "About the wrappers and stuff in your house."

"It was the night I arrived. By the time I knew you well enough to talk about my past, I'd already decided there'd simply been someone staying in the house before I moved in. A squatter or the like. And I can't make sense of it."

"What do you mean?" he asked.

She was puffing a bit and he slowed the pace.

"Whoever Andre sent, assuming it is the motorcyclist, was in my house before I arrived. How would he know I was moving there? And even more perplexing is why he's done nothing to find the USB?"

"Are you sure? What if he's searched the house and is some kind of expert who leaves no trace?"

"He left plenty of trace behind in the cave."

"Probably took a chance nobody would find it. Perhaps he's worked out you carry it with you."

"Then why hasn't he accosted me at home? Or when I'm alone somewhere?"

They reached a small clearing where three tracks met and Kane stopped. He squeezed one of Nellie's hands.

"Thank goodness he hasn't. My concern though is getting you somewhere safe and calling the police. I know you don't want to hear this but the time has come to talk to them. We need help, Nellie."

Her face was drawn and her eyes uncertain but she nodded.

Kane checked his phone for the hundredth time. There was a bar showing so he dialled Bindarra Creek police station. "Nup. Didn't connect."

"Write a text message to Abby. It will send when there's coverage." She took her own phone out. "I'm going to message Cory and ask who his mystery boyfriend is."

"Why?"

"He said he thought he was 'the one' and has always been adamant about falling for an older man with an accent. The man I saw with Andre that night is about fifty and American. I'm probably wrong but..."

"This man? You feel he was a threat to you?"

Her short laugh answered. "He suggested to Andre that he should quote, 'get rid of me' and chased me down several flights of stairs. He's fit. And mean."

Rage roared through Kane but he had to control it. He couldn't frighten Nellie any more than she already was. But if he found himself alone with that man, he wasn't sure he would manage to hold back.

Nellie's fingers closed around his arm and she leaned against him for a moment as if she could see into his mind. The anger drained away.

I just want to protect you.

He needed a clear head. Emotions could wait.

"I want to get you home. My home, where I can feed you and let you rest."

The argument he expected didn't happen. She was more exhausted than she looked to not debate the point. It wasn't a lot further to the camping ground and then only a short walk to his 4WD. And hopefully Abby would get his message and meet them there.

They reached the edge of the ridge above the camping ground and suddenly, both phones pinged.

Nellie undid her pack, letting it drop as she grabbed her phone.

Abby had replied to Kane's message.

> The owner of the motorbike is an ex-armed forces man from the US. Sydney resident. Looking into his background now but suggest keep your distance. Will meet you at Nellie's vehicle.

Kane wanted to grab Nellie and run into the bushes. Who knew what was coming for them? They had nothing to protect themselves apart from whatever might be inside the backpacks and could be re-purposed but at this moment, he had no idea what. He tapped back.

> Nellie is exhausted. Can you bring extra water?

Another message arrived, this time from Blair.

> Sorry it took so long. Flat out with meetings. All I could find out is that Andre Canning had a verbal argument with Carlo Bianchi recently after a charity event. Something about Bianchi's business. Let me know if you want me to dig more.

"Oh, Cory."

With a small sob, Nellie squatted and dropped her head into one of her hands.

"What? What's happened?"

Kane knelt at her side, rubbing her shoulders.

She raised her eyes. "He was dating that man. The one with Andre...Spence. Last time he saw him was two days before I arrived in Glenmeer and since then, Spence has stood him up saying he's out of town. And there's more."

"Sit, Nellie. Take a quick rest."

With a small sigh she adjusted her position to sit on the ground.

"Cory remembers walking in on Spence checking his phone. Spence laughed it off saying he was putting his own phone number and email into it so that Cory would never have an excuse not to find him. And poor Cory thought nothing of it but that must have been when Spence found my number."

"But your address?"

She shrugged. "Andre has friends everywhere. He must have got someone to track it down and looking back, there were other people who might have helped him. The real estate agent obviously knows where I live. And I had to provide a number for the power company."

Below, near the camping ground, there was movement. Kane held his finger up in a 'shh' motion.

A man stood near a motorcycle parked in the middle, open part of the area. His helmet was off and he used binoculars to scope the top of the tree line of the other side of the valley.

Kane gestured to some bushes and they shuffled across, planting themselves on their stomachs on either side of a trunk. They were deep enough in the shade to hide for now but this changed everything. Nellie's SUV wasn't far away but they couldn't risk going anywhere near the man.

"Is that him?" he whispered.

"Yes. Spence."

Spence trained his binoculars in their direction and they flattened themselves.

Nellie was shaking, trembling from head to foot and there was nothing Kane could do other than hold her fingers, the only part he could reach. Their faces were turned to each other and her eyes—which were tightly shut—dripped tears.

Make a plan. Get us out of this.

He couldn't let the feelings and the fear overwhelm him.

The motorcycle roared into life and Nellie squealed.

Kane was on his feet in time to see the direction Spence took and then he had both hands under Nellie's arms, lifting her upright. She swayed in front of him, her face filthy from the dust and tears and her lips open in shock. He put a hand on either side of her face and leaned closer.

"We're going to grab a water bottle each and then we're going to run. Can you do it?"

She nodded and drew in a quick breath. "I'm okay."

"He's making his way up here so we need to move."

Nellie was ahead of him, first to the backpacks. Once they both had water bottles, they stowed the packs in the bushes.

"No point him knowing if we have them." Kane grabbed her hand. "He's not going to find us."

With the sound of the motor fading, they ran along the ridge.

There was a way down but not toward the camping area.

Not to the safety of the SUV and the hope the police were close by.

They were headed into the depths of the National Park.

Chapter Twenty-Eight

Spence turned off the motor when the ridge flattened out.

They weren't here. Of course, they'd be gone thanks to the noise the motorcycle made. But now he knew they weren't far away which was a decent enough trade-off.

Seeing them go into the cave made him sick. Angry-sick. Thanks to this country's pathetic excuse for cell coverage, he'd struggled to identify where Annalise and her boyfriend were heading until it was too late to check he'd not left anything behind in the cave. He'd expected to be back there tonight while he waited...endlessly, for frigging Andre to give him the go-ahead.

Spence got off the bike and gazed around. This was where he'd caught a glimpse of the boyfriend. He pulled his phone out and tapped on the app he'd had custom made. A flashing blip on the screen moved erratically toward the main road. Annalise had no idea. Cory's phone had proved invaluable. He'd never needed her phone number because his app did everything for him. From the first text message between Cory and Annalise he'd known precisely where she was and who she called – even the real estate agent.

As long as she had the phone on her and it was turned on, he'd find her.

Spence sent a message to Andre.

> Now or never, mate. She knows I'm onto her. So does her boyfriend. I need the green light.

The response was immediate.

> What boyfriend?

He laughed. Andre was smart. But stupid when it came to this woman. And was the only reason he'd not got what he came for yet.

> An about-to-be-dead boyfriend.

Back on his bike, he planned his route. He could go almost anywhere a hiker could, bar some of the steeper, rockier parts such as the one those two had taken. To catch up, he had to divert for a few miles.

The phone pinged.

> I want that USB. And her back here. Dispose of the man.

Unsure that he'd bother with the middle instruction, Spence kicked the bike into action.

Chapter Twenty-Nine

Nellie and Kane scrambled down a steep incline, grabbing at bushes to stop themselves losing their footing. Small stones flew ahead from the disturbance and a flock of cockatoos rose from a tree with furious screeching. Kane glanced up at them.

"Wait on, Nellie."

Easier said than done.

She put the brakes on too fast and ended up on her behind and scraping her palms on the rough surface.

"You okay?"

Kane opened his water bottle.

"Hold them out."

She turned her palms up and he poured a bit of water over them.

"Why did we stop?" Nellie panted as she shook her hands.

"The birds." Kane pointed to where the group circled. "Anyone seeing them would know we disturbed them. Spence has to find another way down unless he goes on foot so we could have taken things a bit less chaotically."

"Where are we going? I feel so lost."

"Not lost. Can you see that over there?" He gestured to a towering formation. Nellie had noticed it from almost everywhere they'd been today. "That's Eagle Rock and we're going roughly in the opposite direction. If it was earlier in the day, we'd head around it and get to Tulachmhor, to the Sullivan's. Reid would be the first to help us."

Climbing to her feet, Nellie started off again, toward the huge rock.

"No, Nellie."

If she didn't do something she'd cry and that was pathetic and not helpful. But she stopped again as he caught up, his arm slipping around her shoulders.

He held her against him. "I don't think we can cover that distance before nightfall."

"We have our phones. We can use their torches."

"Which might lead our two wheeled friend to us. And there's a river to cross unless we can get to a bridge." He shook his head and dropped his arm. "We're close enough to Mt. Ingalls Road to get there using fire trails in the remaining daylight. But we can't run, I was wrong to say that."

She gazed at his face, every bit as dusty and strained as she imagined hers was. Exhaustion in his eyes reflected her own, but she wasn't going to give up. She'd brought this danger to Glenmeer, to Kane. She had to fix it. Andre wouldn't let her come to any harm...at least not until he got what he wanted. Nellie touched the pendant.

I'll do anything to keep you safe, Kane.

He was tapping on his phone and she checked hers. Before she could stop herself, she wrote a message.

Meet me face to face and I'll hand over the
USB. But no Spence. No hurting anyone.
This is a one-time offer, Andre.

She added a location just outside Bindarra Creek and
made a time tomorrow afternoon, then changed the phone
to vibrate only.

"Nellie?"

"Um, no coverage. Did you message Abby?" She slid the
phone into her pocket.

He was frowning. Did he suspect what she was
planning?

"I've let her know where we're heading. Are you okay?"

With a nod, she touched his arm. "Can we get going?"

The next few minutes were quiet as they weaved
around trees and waded through a small creek. Birds
settling for the evening was the only constant sound, and it
was a relief. Soon they'd be on a proper road and even if the
police weren't there, might be able to flag down a lift.
Nellie's legs ached and her feet were almost numb but as
soon as that message went, she'd feel safe again. Safer.

They were climbing again but only a gradual rise.
Almost at the top, Kane put a hand on her arm and they
stopped. Listening. Nothing.

"Just ahead is a fire trail. There was one at the bottom of
the ridge but we've gone away at an arc."

"Why would we do that? Wouldn't a fire trail be easier
to follow?" Nellie opened her water bottle. There wasn't a
lot left.

"It would. But Spence would have found it pretty easily
and I reckon he's hooning around the bush on it. Pity it'll
take him toward the river and the guest house sitting up
there." Kane grinned. "He's been out here a while and will

have done his research about the park. The guest house is a safe spot, and it makes sense we'd go there."

"And this fire trail leads to the road?"

"It does."

His phone beeped, and hers vibrated in her pocket.

"I'm going to visit a tree. Okay?" She mustered a smile for the term she'd been using to have privacy to relieve herself and when Kane nodded, checking his phone, she slipped away into the undergrowth. There was a reply from Andre.

I'll be there.

She messaged back.

Call off Spence or no deal.

The three dots moved then stopped. Moved again. And stopped.

"Come on, come on," she whispered.

"All okay? No drop bears?"

"Very funny. Be right back."

I've told him. Very disappointed in you, Annalise.

Her fingers worked faster than her brain.

In me? Look in a mirror, Andre.

This time the response was fast.

You still haven't got a clue. The business doesn't matter, only vengeance. Carlo crossed me and now I'm taking his precious business.

Be there tomorrow.

Be there.

There was so much she wanted to say and her fingers hovered above the phone.

"Nellie, we have to go now."

The phone went back into her pocket.

Chapter Thirty

Something was going on with Nellie but Kane had no idea how to broach the subject without sounding suspicious of her nor had the brain power to work it out. She was too interested in her phone, considering the poor reception and her knowing he was keeping in contact with Abby—when coverage allowed.

He was stopping them both too much and could sense her increasing agitation, but had to be certain of following the right trails. They'd moved from one to another and now were on their third, cutting across bushland to find the next and the next.

"You didn't tell me if you heard from Abby."

And you haven't told me who messaged you. Several times.

He'd heard the phone vibrate. Perhaps that was what put his senses on high alert because until then, her phone—like his—had beeped with a message.

"Careful around here, there's a number of sharp rocks just beneath the surface."

"Okay."

Nellie was close behind, her feet following his.

"I did. She has called for more units to come and help and will patrol up and down Mt. Ingalls Road looking for us."

"She can't drive up the fire trail?"

"She could. But what if it's the wrong one?"

Nellie didn't respond, and he reached back for her hand, which slipped into his. Once they got past this mess, he was going to ask her out on a proper date and take her to visit his mother.

As long as we get out of this.

Thank goodness Nellie hadn't seen what he had. The gun holster worn by that man, Spence. So much she'd kept from him. Who sends an armed man to stalk someone? What was really behind this whole drama, because there had to be more to it than one person's desire to build a business empire.

"Kane?"

All he needed was ten minutes—heck, one minute alone with this Andre Canning.

"Kane, stop, please."

He did.

And immediately heard what she had.

"Duck down. He won't see us here."

They got as low to the ground as possible, tucked behind bushes again. Thank goodness for the dense Australian landscape.

The motorcycle was going slowly and in a straight line. Its headlight was on.

Rookie mistake.

There was still enough light to see a fair distance ahead but Spence was struggling. Kane's eyes were well accustomed to the early evening shift in light. Particularly out here, where the majestic gums filtered the sun, turning it into a mix of green and grey shaded light which someone unused to it might find difficult.

"He's on the trail that we are going onto next."

"So, we need to change direction."

Nellie's voice was flat. She had to be completely wiped. Almost a full day of hiking in sometimes difficult terrain and then fleeing from danger. And the swimming.

One beautiful highlight.

"Hey," he whispered, smiling when she turned her face in question. "Any other time I'd suggest we go back to the pool and swim beneath the stars."

Her expression softened, her eyes bright with whatever her own memories and feelings were about their earlier experience.

"And we will. If you want to."

She leaned into him. "A midnight picnic?"

"We can even take a giant pink flamingo Lilo if you'd like."

Nellie giggled and suddenly, all was right in his world.

"No? Okay, what about a—"

Her lips crushed against his and whatever silly suggestion he'd come up with was gone from his mind. He returned the kiss until the sound of the motorcycle intruded and she pulled away, leaving him bereft of her warmth.

Spence was riding back. Now he had a wide torch and slowly moved it from side to side of the fire trail. It flashed on the tree near them but they were well out of sight and neither of them moved an inch.

He passed and the grumble of the motor receded.

"Ready to make a run for it?" Kane asked.

"Do you mean run this time?"

Fair question.

"Let's walk to the fire trail and then we'll make an executive decision."

Chapter Thirty-One

There was no doubt Kane knew his stuff.

Nellie had absolute trust that he'd get them to safety.

And then I can ensure his future safety.

Kissing him as they'd hidden behind the bushes confirmed what she'd been denying for a while. In a ridiculously short time, she'd fallen head over heels in love with Kane Maxwell.

Accepting it brought out instincts she'd forgotten. Until being old enough to see her mother for the selfish woman she was, Nellie had loved her unconditionally and done everything she knew how to protect her. Even as a child. Moving in with her eccentric father, she'd done the same. Watching out for him all the time until he'd simply disappeared to pursue yet another romance. Now she had Kane. He'd done nothing but care for her since the beginning. He'd welcomed her into his life and that of his family and friends. Given her a safe place to stay. Been her friend. And made her laugh and feel more than she'd ever experienced.

Now it was her job to protect him from Andre.

"This trail will take us directly to Mt. Ingalls Road. If

absolutely necessary, we could cut across country from it and get to my house," Kane said.

He held her hand as they stood on the edge of the bush-land. One step forward and they'd be on what was a decent track, cleared enough for a fire truck to fit and well main-tained. This was where Spence had cruised up and down and then moved on.

"What if he comes back?"

"The beauty of him riding that thing is the noise it makes. We hear it and we go bush again. Things have altered with dusk. This is my territory and this man—ex-armed forces or not—is clearly not equipped for the Australian bush. Can you jog for a bit?"

"Can you keep up?" Nellie flashed a smile at Kane then dashed away.

"Other direction."

She did a U-turn and passed him. "You *are* good at this."

It only took a few strides for him to catch her and they settled into a slow run, side by side. Knowing they were so close to safety had lifted her spirits and increased her energy.

Her phone vibrated as they reached a cross road.

"Let's stop for sec and I'll see if there's anything from Abby."

Nellie reached for her own phone and froze. "Do you hear that?"

In an instant Kane had grabbed her hand and was almost dragging her into the undergrowth. Her water bottle flew out of her grasp, bouncing off the ground and spinning away.

The motorcycle roared as it approached.

"Down."

They were a few metres from the trail, behind a fallen

tree. How did he know where they were? Something had to be bringing him back down this track time and again.

She pulled her phone out and glared at it.

"What?"

"It has to be my phone. Maybe he can find it somehow."

"Take the sim card and battery out."

Her hands were shaking too much. "I can't. And you need something to poke in it to eject the sim on this. Throw it far away, Kane."

She pushed the offending phone at him.

"We might never find it again."

The motorcycle came to a stop a little further along the road and turned off.

"Annalise! You can't hide forever so let's make a deal."

Nellie covered her mouth with her hands as the same voice who'd told Andre to get rid of her those months ago carried from perhaps fifty metres away.

"So, here's the deal. You come out from wherever you and your boyfriend are hiding and give me that USB."

His voice drifted closer. He must be moving. Walking.

"In return, I won't kill you. Either of you. We'll part ways as friends."

Her throat constricted, and she lowered her hands to let more air in.

Crunch.

"Lookie see. A water bottle. You think you can hide from me?" Spence laughed loudly. "Not while there's cell coverage you can't."

She was right.

Kane's lips were beside her ear. "When he moves, I want you to get onto the trail again and keep going until you hit the main road. Hide until I find you or Abby does." He kissed her cheek. When she turned to say no, she didn't want him to go...he already had. Only the movement of the fond of a tree fern gave away that anyone had passed.

All was silent except the pounding of her heart.

She couldn't even see the road from here, so dense was the undergrowth. Spence might be a metre away and she wouldn't know until it was too late. But if she walked onto the fire trial right now and told him she'd made an arrangement with Andre, then he'd have to honour it. He'd have to talk to Andre at the very least and that would buy time for the police to find them.

Spence swore.

A few seconds later the motorcycle roared into life and moved away.

Nellie worked her way to the edge of the fire trail. The motorcycle was going the opposite direction.

She launched herself onto the track and ran for her life.

Chapter Thirty-Two

Follow me, you monster.

Kane weaved between trees and jumped over fallen branches, getting away from Mt. Ingalls Road and the fire trail. When he heard the engine kick in, he took it up a notch.

Nellie had to get to safety. She was right about the phone otherwise why would Spence be behind him now?

He aimed for the highest ground he could see in the hope the coverage wouldn't drop out. It meant being out in the open for a couple of seconds to cross another fire trail and he managed to reach the other side just as the motorcycle rounded a curve. He was certain he'd not been seen.

The problem was that no matter how fast he was, the terrain was difficult. And his pursuer was much faster for as long as the motorcycle could manage the bush.

Sweat poured down his face and back.

The muscles in his legs screamed at him to slow down. They'd been tested too much this afternoon.

Not until Nellie is safe.

There was no way to tell for sure but she only needed a

few minutes running at speed to reach Mt. Ingalls Road. By drawing Spence away, he was buying her time.

Kane burst into a clearing. To one side was the forest, and the other dropped away steeply. There were boulders and he leaped from one to another, going higher until he reached the top and then he listened.

No motorcycle. Had the man alighted and followed on foot?

The phone vibrated and instinctively he turned it to see the message.

> Spence isn't answering his phone so I can't call him off. I'd be running, Annalise.

"Stop! Annalise we can fix this."

"Not a chance." With all his might, Kane flung the phone away from himself into the dark void below.

Chapter Thirty-Three

Cars zipped past, their headlights too bright for Nellie to tell if they were friend or foe. A motorcycle roared down the road and she dived back into the bushes, heart beating so fast she thought she'd pass out.

It was dark now. She had no idea how long she'd been here. How long since Kane left, and she'd run until her legs gave out and her lungs burned. She'd lost her bearings but when the road quieted again and she forced her mind to focus, Nellie figured she could find her way home. But what if Spence was waiting for her? He might not have fallen for Kane's ruse.

Why was he still after her?

Andre said he'd call him off but hadn't. Or else, Spence ignored him.

All she had was the pendant and the precious information it contained.

But all she *wanted* was Kane.

She ached for him.

Squatting behind a tree trunk, Nellie had no idea what to do. She could try to get home. Or follow the road to Glenmeer and hope one of the residents would answer a knock on their door. Didn't Gigi live behind her home?

But what if I put them in danger as well?

Another set of headlights approached, and this car wasn't zooming along at a hundred kilometres an hour.

They were looking for something.

Someone.

The vehicle passed her, and she ran onto the road, chasing it, arms waving.

It stopped, blue and red lights on top turning on and the driver climbing out.

Nellie almost fell against the back of the paddy wagon.

"Hey, hey. We're here."

"Abby. You need to find Kane. He's in terrible danger."

There was another police officer as well and as he and Abby reached Nellie, her legs betrayed her and she crumpled to the ground.

Chapter Thirty-Four

"I don't need an ambulance." Nellie insisted for the third time. Nobody else agreed, and she reluctantly sank onto the spot the paramedic gestured on a step behind the ambulance. "Besides, why are you even here? Nobody is hurt."

Abby had just hung up a phone call and must have overheard. She said something to her partner and came to Nellie.

So much had happened since she'd been found. The ambulance arrived minutes later, as well as a patrol car. Abby had been on the phone and in discussion with the other officers and the second car had just left to stop traffic coming from Glenmeer. Nellie had heard mention of more units coming from the Armidale direction and they'd also make a barrier. She'd been plied with water and blurted out the information about Kane and Spence.

She began to shiver.

The paramedic noticed and draped a silver fabric over her shoulders.

"Shock, Nellie. At the very least, so please do whatever the paramedic says. Ambulance is here because Kane texted me that the motorcyclist is carrying a gun. Thank goodness he didn't use it but you are going to be checked out before you go too far. Okay?"

Abby smiled to soften the directive and Nellie nodded. Her legs were too shaky for her to go too far and there was a ridiculous urge to cry her eyes out which she barely controlled.

"What about...Kane?"

"Kane knows the park and it being night time won't bother him. The minute another unit arrives, we're driving up the trail you came down."

Nellie's head pounded and her gut churned. What if Spence had caught up with Kane? Surely, he should be here by now.

"I have to go, Nellie. Talk to the paramedic if you need anything." Abby squeezed Nellie's shoulder and hurried the dozen steps to the paddy wagon.

It was surreal sitting here on the back of an ambulance on the side of the main road only a few metres from the entry to the fire trail.

Overhead, the night sky had a glorious display of stars and with only the occasional car passing toward Glenmeer, there was quiet for the most part. But Nellie's heart was breaking with each passing moment.

Where are you, Kane?

If she'd known it would come to this...if she'd had an inkling she'd fall in love and put that person in the sights of a dangerous man...if anything happened to Kane, it was her fault.

The only mistake you've made is not going to the police.

She played with the pendant. Was it time to come clean about this and get help? Or keep her meeting with Andre tomorrow and get him out of her life for good? But then, what about Carlo? There had to be a way to fix everything. Nellie's shoulders drooped. But how?

A motorcycle approached. Well, the sound of it did, the motor exactly like Spence's. But it couldn't be, could it?

"He's right behind me!"

Kane flew around the corner from the fire trail and raced around the paddy wagon.

Abby and the other officer drew their weapons as they ran to the narrow track.

"Kane!" Nellie screamed as she scrambled to her feet. "I'm here."

Even as he covered the short distance to her, tears of pure relief poured down her cheeks and then she was in his arms. He dripped with sweat and didn't smell the best but she didn't care one bit as he picked her up and planted a kiss on her lips.

"Watch out!"

Voices yelled as the motorcycle skidded past the police, leaning to one side, its tyres screeching under duress. Still holding Nellie up against himself, Kane swung them both to the safe side of the ambulance and straight into a ditch where he ended on top of her.

A loud bang shook the air as glass and metal crumbled against the tarmac.

For a moment there was absolute silence. And then raised voices and cries of agony and people running.

"We might stay put for a minute. You okay?"

"Well, the ditch is filled with itchy grass and weeds. I think your knee is on top of my leg—oh that's better, thanks. And I can't see anything."

"What do you mean? Did you hit your head?"

Kane went to get up and Nellie grabbed his face. "Tears. Just tears, Kane. I thought he'd killed you."

His body relaxed. "No more tears. I think Spence might have had a little accident and is probably in an awful lot of trouble. And I was never in danger because two strong legs and knowledge of the local terrain beats a thug on a motorbike any day of the week."

The cries of pain changed to foul language from Spence and stern instructions from Abby.

"She's awesome," Nellie said.

Kane had brushed away most of the tears on her face and stared at her as though she was the most precious thing he'd ever seen. Electricity sparked up and down her body and the heat from his body warmed her more than the silver fabric. Far more. Her heart was galloping, and all she wanted was another kiss.

"I love you," she whispered.

It was the right moment to tell him. He had to know before he disappeared into the bushland again or put his life at risk for her.

"Nellie, there's something we need to talk about."

I just told you how I feel. Did you not hear me?

"Kane, I—"

"Told you we'd need an ambulance." A light flashed into the ditch. "Handy that your mate over there crashed near one," Abby said. "Are you stuck in the ditch?"

"Needed a little rest." Kane climbed to his feet and reached for Nellie.

She shook his hands off, ignoring the confusion in his face as she straightened. What she'd said was a mistake. He had heard her and was about to say he didn't feel the same when they were interrupted. But why did his eyes say otherwise? And his lips, whenever he kissed her?

"May I go home, Abby?"

"Get some rest and we'll do an interview tomorrow. Give me a few minutes and I'll get a lift for you both."

Nellie began to shiver again and Kane wrapped his arms around her.

This time she let him and closed her eyes, knowing she should tell him she was fine but just for a little while she needed to pretend he loved her as well.

Chapter Thirty-Five

Kane gripped the steering wheel, leaning forward a bit to spot the turn to the carpark where they'd left Nellie's SUV yesterday. "Almost there. Then we'll head to Bindarra Creek."

"I don't know how long I'll be at the police station. Might even get arrested."

Her voice was light but her face—still drawn and tired —had that worried look Kane had got too accustomed to seeing.

"Only people being arrested are Spence and Andre."

Kane had stayed at Nellie's house overnight once he and the police officer who'd dropped them off checked the property. A quick visit home for fresh clothes and he'd been back to settle into the spare bedroom after a much-needed shower and late dinner they'd thrown together.

The sun was only just up when they'd turned onto Mt. Ingalls Road away from Glenmeer after a quick breakfast.

"You know we need to talk, Nellie."

"Oh, there's the turn off."

"Thank you. We can't pretend I don't know you were communicating with Andre yesterday."

Nellie flashed him a quick smile. "Next time you are about to throw someone's phone into the depth of a valley, don't read their messages and then you won't worry."

"Not funny."

"It will be okay."

Not until Andre is arrested and you are free to start living again.

She said nothing more, watching out the window until they reached her vehicle. After climbing out she gazed around and with a small gasp, put her hand over her mouth.

"What's wrong?"

She dropped her hand. "All the photos. May I borrow your phone for a minute?"

He handed it over. Of course, she'd be upset at losing the beautiful images she'd taken. "We can retrace our steps. When you're ready."

Nellie scrolled through his phone with a small smile. "Not to that cave though. Look." She turned the phone to a picture of the pool, sunlight glinting off the water. "I was uploading to the gallery on your website as I was going but with the shonky coverage thought I'd lost the lot."

Her eyes shone and his heart flipped over and he couldn't help himself. Kane gently pulled her into his arms and kissed her.

He'd heard her words last night while his body sheltered her from whatever was going on near the ambulance. All he'd longed to do was tell her how much he loved her in return. But knowing she'd reached out to Andre put his feelings on the back burner. She'd obviously asked the man to stop Spence and Andre had agreed but been unable to fulfil his side of whatever bargain they'd brokered.

As her fingers ran through his hair to pull him closer, none of that mattered.

At this moment, they were a couple in love.

Nothing will get between us.

Nellie broke the kiss. "We're being watched," she whispered.

Kane's head shot around to where she was looking and he laughed as a mob of curious kangaroos inched closer.

Correction, nothing apart from giant hopping creatures.

"I'd better get going, anyway," she said. "See what the police have to say about all of this."

"Shall I go first?"

"Probably best in case I take the wrong turn. Still getting to know this area." Nellie reached up to deliver one last kiss.

On the road to Bindarra Creek, Kane glanced often into his side mirrors. Nellie's vehicle was behind him the whole time. They both had police interviews to attend and then... well, time would tell.

Chapter Thirty-Six

A few kilometres from Bindarra Creek on the way to Tamworth, Nellie pulled into a deserted roadside stop. There was a gazebo of sorts with no sides and a tin roof sheltering a couple of tables with attached benches. The ground was red dirt in the carpark with scattered clumps of grass dotted around. Gum trees and a handful of banksia bushes offered some privacy around the back of the gazebo and there was a small toilet block and a water tank close by. It was set back from the main road but from where she parked, cars and trucks were still visible as they zipped by.

She was confident she'd not been followed.

For a minute or two she didn't move, gripping the steering wheel as her heart thudded. Assuming Andre kept their meeting, he'd be here soon. Would he bring another thug to back him up? Or a weapon? She'd learned much about him since running for her life.

Nellie pushed the door open and climbed out. She'd stay away from her vehicle and his in case he tried to force her to go with him.

It's just a transaction. He'll want to leave once he has the USB.

Telling herself that didn't help.

There was nothing about Andre Canning she understood anymore, apart from his single-minded need to get his hands on another man's company. No matter who was hurt in the process.

A car slowed and nosed toward her car.

Nellie moved to the gazebo.

It was Andre.

She glanced around at the trees and bushes. The toilet block and water tank. No sign of anyone being here other than the two of them.

He got out of his car and stared at her across its roof.

Hold your ground. This is almost over.

"All that gorgeous hair of yours is gone, Annalise. Yet, you're still as stunning as the last time I saw you."

Andre wandered around the car. No designer suit, just sunglasses, jeans, and T-shirt. Any other time...once upon a time, Nellie would have taken a moment to admire him. So self-assured, handsome, even funny.

Except now I know you are none of those.

"How did you get away from Spence? He'd complained about poor cell tower coverage over the past couple of weeks but he must have got the message. After all, here you are in one piece." He stepped beneath the gazebo and stopped, taking his sunglasses off and hooking them on the front of his T-shirt.

"Hasn't he been in touch since last night?" Nellie asked, knowing the answer.

"What, did you and the new boyfriend push him off his motorbike?"

"Didn't need to. He fell off all by himself going around a

corner too fast. Must have been shocked at the sight of the police waiting for him." There was no way for her to hold in a smirk. "I wonder what he's told them?"

Andre's eyes hardened and one of his hands clenched into a fist.

"You didn't know that the man you sent to kill me is in custody?" she asked.

"I didn't send him to kill you, Annalise. I sent him to retrieve my property which you stole. Why you even did is beyond me. We had a great relationship. I did so much for your career."

"He was in my home, Andre. Probably multiple times. He followed me and watched me and came after me with a gun."

Andre took a couple of steps and Nellie placed herself on the opposite side of the table and benches. He stopped again, an unpleasant sneer turning his good looks ugly. "His choice. I instructed him to bring me back the USB. Up to him how he achieved it."

"And yet, he didn't."

Nellie's legs were like water and if she had to run, it was doubtful she'd get too far. Had he said enough yet?

"I have a flight back to Sydney to catch and quite honestly, didn't appreciate being dragged up here. Only decent small plane is a corporate jet, not the thing I flew into Tamworth on so hand it over, Annalise."

"And then what?"

"I go back to Sydney and you get to live a long and boring life here."

Boring? I will settle for it.

"What happens with the contents of the USB?" She wanted to hear him say it.

"I'm finally going to get what I want. Ownership of one

of the country's premier talent agencies and long overdue revenge." Andre held out his hand. "No more wasting my time."

She slid the pendant over her head and placed it onto the table, backing a few feet as he grabbed at it. He held it aloft and then pulled it apart, tossing the chain and outer casing onto the ground. "That wasn't so hard, was it?" Andre tucked the USB into a pocket in his jeans and turned to walk away.

"Do you really think Carlo will give in to blackmail?" Nellie asked. "He might call your bluff or go to the police."

Still walking, Andre shook his head. "Not unless he wants to lose his wife and kids. And his fortune." Now, he turned around, planting his feet with a sinister grin on his face. "Let alone his reputation. In fact, it is the one thing he cares about the most. And this little thing," he patted his pocket, "has the power to destroy everything he values. So yes, he will give in to blackmail. All you did by stealing it was delay the inevitable."

"What did he ever do to you?"

"Not that it's any of your business, but his wife? The one he's cheating on? She was my fiancé until he came along. Seems like karma that now I get to take his company."

Nellie nodded. "Thank you, Andre."

"For what?"

She didn't need to look at him anymore. As she walked in the opposite direction, he spluttered.

"Where the hell are you going?"

To the other side of the trees. To the back of the water tank.

Several uniformed police officers rushed out from behind the toilet block.

"Andre Canning, put your hands behind your head and lock your fingers."

The yelling of police and Andre faded as Nellie sprinted away.

To the man I love.

Kane appeared from the back of the water tank, his arms wrapping around her in an instant. Her legs buckled, and he lifted her and whisked them both to behind some trees, out of sight of the chaos of the arrest near the cars.

"I just got the shakes, I'm okay." Her voice came out as a shaky laugh. "Adrenaline."

His eyes searched her face.

"Truly. I need some water and to sit for a few minutes."

"But then I can't do this."

He kissed her, a long, deep exploration of her mouth which took her breath away and left her senses spinning.

Then, he set her down and sat with her.

"I'll get you some water soon. You did it."

She leaned against the trunk of the tree, holding one of his hands with both of hers as relief seeped into every part of her. "They heard everything?"

"Sure did. But they also complained about you choosing a spot like this to meet him. Nowhere for the vehicles to be hidden."

"I didn't expect to have to cater for anyone else."

"No. No, Nellie, you were going to come here alone and risk your life." Kane's voice was growly. "He might have killed you." He pulled his hand out of hers and ran it through his hair. "I can't lose you." His expression softened as he gazed at her. "I love you."

A lump of pure joy stuck in her throat until she gulped it down.

"I love you too. And I feel the same. I told Andre to call

Spence off if he wanted the USB and he agreed. But when Spence kept coming and then you disappeared...I felt as though my heart would break. And that is why I told Abby everything this morning." She held out her hand. "Today was all about putting things right even if it meant facing that man again. I am so sorry I worried you."

"Worried?" Kane took a long, deep breath and then laced his fingers with hers. "Aged me ten years."

"Good thing I like older men."

Kane's shoulders visibly relaxed. "Not too much older. Like, not Andre older?"

"Ew."

"Okay then."

Nellie snuggled against Kane, listening to the steady beat of his heart. There was nothing boring about her new life. Not that she wanted to live through the past few months again, but there was a certain excitement, a danger in the unknown risks of starting over. And between the unchartered parts of the National Park she'd explore, and the depths of the love she'd found, it was a perfect danger.

Epilogue

"You know, Nellie, he had a thing about you from the first time you met...not met as such. But when you gazed at each other across the distance between your respective drive-ways, he just knew." Blair ducked as Kane threw a tea towel at his head. "Missed."

"Just knew what?" Nellie scooped up the tea towel. "That I'd put him into a situation where his life was at risk? And he'd have to lead a criminal with murderous intent on a chase through the park in darkness? Or that he'd have to give evidence in an upcoming trial?"

"He knew you were the one for him. You see, Kane's a nice enough fellow but lacking in a few areas—"

"I beg your pardon?" Kane spluttered.

"Might be good at stomping around the National Park but very few people skills and not really the brightest. He needed a smart and kind person to see past his flaws. Someone who can make him look good."

Nellie threw the tea towel and didn't miss. It ended up covering Blair's face.

"Much better," Kane said. "Tell us again why you're here, little brother?"

"Because he misses me." Miranda wandered in from the outdoors entertainment area, where a table was set up for an evening meal. "And I can see why he misses me." She slowly removed the tea towel and kissed his lips. "A few weeks back in Sydney and his maturity level drops. Good thing I love you."

"Old man outside starving to death." Pop's plaintive call drifted in. Tangles, who sat beside Pop at the table, barked in agreement and everyone laughed.

Kane picked up a tray of drinks. "We've been told."

The last couple of weeks were, without doubt, the best of his life. Once the police statements were out of the way, Andre and Spence under arrest, and the cloud of fear and worry lifted from Nellie's shoulders, she'd come alive. Watching her tease Blair only served to make him fall a little bit more in love.

The meal underway, Blair returned to his earlier subject. "So, Nellie. Did Kane mention he took to watching your house at night?"

"Oh my goodness, mate. Give it a rest."

Nellie's eyes sparkled. "I want to hear."

Kane put his hand up as Blair took a breath. "Eat your carrots, junior. The truth is that the second night you were in your house I was putting the rubbish out and heard you cry out. It was obvious the power wasn't connected so I headed to the fence in case you'd fallen or something but then an almighty light shone in my direction. Surprised you didn't see me."

Spearing a piece of potato, she grinned. "I did. Well, I saw something and wondered if the region was known for some kind of mythical creature in white."

Blair had a deflated expression as he munched on a carrot roasted in honey, butter, and black pepper. Miranda patted his arm, barely able to contain her amusement. Pop just shook his head and snuck some green beans under the table for Tangles.

"Back to my question from in the kitchen, Blair...why the trip home so soon after heading back to Sydney? I mean, you are welcome of course but it's a long drive just for dinner."

All eyes, apart from Nellie's—who was concentrating on her meal—turned to Kane. Nobody said a word and eventually Nellie noticed and glanced up.

"What am I supposed to know?" Why did they all look so serious?

"Son, you and Nellie could have died out there," Pop said.

Miranda nodded. "When we heard what happened, you have no idea how worried we were."

"Had to come and see for myself you were okay." Blair mumbled into a napkin.

Kane's eyes moved from one to the other. He hadn't realised and yet, he should have known. "We're fine though. Really, we were in less danger than the local newspaper made out. And the police were terrific."

Nellie pushed back her chair and stood. "I'm...I'm so sorry. None of this would have happened if I hadn't come here." With that, she burst into tears and ran inside. Tangles tore off after her.

She hadn't gone far, just to the kitchen. Kane wrapped his arms around her and let her sob against his chest. And then Blair was there, adding his arms around them both, and Pop, and Miranda. They huddled together while Tangles tried to squeeze between their legs.

"Sweetie, nobody blames you," Kane said.

"Besides, we're also talking about Caryn," Blair said. "That is a whole different level of scary."

"You aren't to blame, Nellie, dear," Pop said. "You did the right thing to stop bad people. And if you hadn't moved here, we wouldn't have the pleasure of knowing you."

"Or loving you." Kane kissed her cheek. "And nobody is letting go of you until you tell us it wasn't your fault."

Nellie giggled. "It is getting kind of hot in the middle."

"Say it, Nellie, then we can have a glass of wine," Miranda said.

"I give up. It wasn't my fault."

One by one, Pop, Miranda, and Blair dropped their arms and stepped away but Kane kept Nellie encircled in his. "No more tears. Not about this. And no more blaming yourself."

With a deep sigh, Nellie relaxed against him.

"Was that a yes?"

"Yes."

"In that case, I'm going back to eat. Feeling weak with hunger," Pop said.

In a moment they were alone. Even Tangles had gone outside again. Kane took Nellie's hand and led her through the house, onto the front verandah.

They sat on the top step, gazing at the night sky with its myriad of brilliant stars. In the distance, a night bird called and a warm breeze rustled the leaves of the gum trees. Laughter drifted from the back of the house and then someone put on some music.

"I think it will take me a while to really believe what I said in there," Nellie said. She shifted a little to look at Kane. "Even though I know it was right to stop Andre harming Carlo, the way I went about it could have been handled better. I've just always had to manage on my own."

"Not now. No more being alone unless you choose to be." Kane's fingers brushed back her hair. "We'll go and visit your mother soon and Cory. Let them know they are always welcome here because now you have a bigger family. One which will never let you down and never let you forget how much we love you."

Her eyes glistened and her face radiated joy.

"I love Blair, even if he is silly sometimes, and Pop and Miranda and Tangles. And I loved spending time with your parents the other day. I never imagined I'd be surrounded by so much love."

Kane brushed his lips against hers. "I love you, An-Nellie. Now and always."

"I love you, Kane. And whatever is ahead, I want to face it at your side."

She leaned against him and his arm went around her shoulders.

A shooting star burned across the sky.

There were no wishes to be made. Everything that mattered was right here.

Excerpt of Amulet of Death

AMULET OF DEATH © SUZANNE GILCHRIST

Sydney Barracks,

16th October, 1914.

Dear family,

Many happy returns, mother and may God grant you many more. Alfred and I are going strong. Do try and not worry. Tell father not to hire Roaming Jack for shearing this year. Too many bloodied sheep the last time he was on our farm. There is plenty of tucker although it is always the same. Nothing like your home cooking mother which I miss dearly. Like our tucker our days are the same. We rise at dawn, march from the barracks to Rosebery, no idea why and back again. There is bayonet practise and we exercise constantly. I suppose we must be in tiptop shape so we can fight the Jerries. Rumour is our squad will leave our shores in the next week or two. It will be bonzers to be on our way. I have taken up learning French, it may prove useful. I am sure we will be home by Christmas.

With love to all, I remain your affect. son and brother, Mitchell.

Exultation sizzled like an electric current through the man's veins as he stepped off the lowest tread of the rickety stairs and into the gloomy cellar. The old timber creaked underfoot, a thunderbolt of noise in the heavy silence. He paused, his breathing pulsing loud in his ears as he sucked in the stink of mould from years of neglect and damp. His excitement heightened, twisting hard in the pit of his gut and his palms tingled. All those years of study and chasing down every clue no matter how small had led him right to this moment, this place. Finally, he was close to achieving his life-long obsession.

He groped along the grimy wall, unable to find another light switch. Slipping his mobile out from his pants' pocket, he flicked on the torch app, then frowned. Layers of cobwebs clung to the ceiling. Mice droppings mounded in the corners. There were no prints in the thick dust underfoot.

No one had entered the cellar in years.

Not that he intended to give up and turn tail now. Everything he'd earned in life had been done the hard way which, in turn, had honed his ruthless nature into a brutal and unrelenting weapon. His prize was close – he knew it, and all he had to do was find the clue that would reveal the next link.

He paced further away from the only other light source, a single bulb positioned above the steep stairs, and pushed aside a curtain of sticky, filmy, web. Just as well cramped, dark places didn't bother him. That particular fear had been well and truly conquered years ago – a time in his life that had essentially gone down to the wire – either deal with it or be broken. He had too much innate stubbornness for that to ever happen. A cockroach skittered across the floor and disappeared beneath a broken sideboard. There were a couple of ancient beer barrels stacked against one wall. Three rickety shelving units stood crammed together, blocking any further passage to the right. He had hoped for at least an old tin trunk or a pile of bric-a-brac to examine.

Nothing. His elation faded. But there were still the old woman's private rooms to search. He'd turn the place inside out if he had to. All he needed was time alone.

A warm puff of air wafted over the back of his bare neck – a sudden odd intrusion in the coldness of the silent cellar. It felt like - *like a breath!*

Like someone was behind him.

His heart slammed against his ribs in a sudden gallop as panic flooded his mind. He stiffened. Whirling thoughts crashed in frantic union with his pounding heart. How could he explain what he was doing prowling about in the cellar? But wait – no one was home. He'd made certain they had all left before he began his search. Then who the dickens stood behind him in weighted silence?

The chill in the cellar increased sending goosebumps brushing over his skin in a flurry of icy strokes. He shivered as the freezing air sank into his bones. Should he attempt to explain? Or wait for the other to speak first? To his left, there was a flick of a tail as a mouse melted into the darkness as if desperate to escape impending danger. His hand tightened around his mobile. But...

A shadow rippled over the wall – *too late*.

A rush of air behind him – *too late*.

Agony splintered across his skull as lethal as a rockslide. His vision dimmed to blackness and he crashed to the floor.

Clan McEwan,

At sea.

3rd July, 1915.

Dear mother and father,

I hope all is well at home. We have been at sea for almost three weeks and at first I was sick as a dog as the old tub rolled all over the place. I am tip top now and we are due to dock in some port or other soon. The tucker is not very plentiful. We only get enough jam and butter to last one meal. But there is enough feed for the horses. Most days, I look after Blaze and Smarty. Tell Matilda they are in fine shape. We had a wash day parade Friday. Shower day is every second day and our water ration is getting smaller. We do drills on the deck. I could do without all the marching as it is very hot. I have not got any letters from you or Alfred and Mitch for some time. What the deuce is going on. Silly beggars. They should have joined the 6th like me and not the 8th. Still I carnt wait to catch up with them in Gallipoli. How are things at home. Do not worry too much, mother. The fellows are a good mob and keen as mustard to fight for our King. We will soon have the Turks on the run. I will close now as the light is fading.

Love to you all from your affect. son, Gregory.

Two coffees and one bottle of water down and Natalie's brekkie *'date'* still hadn't arrived. Seated at one of the Cyprus Café's outside tables gave her a good view of Main Street and she craned her neck for the umpteenth time. However, there was no sign of a silver-haired man amidst the smattering of shoppers trudging along, all rugged up against the wintry morn. Shivering, she swallowed the last mouthful of cold coffee. The excess of caffeine smashed through her system, causing her already jittery nerves to overload. She couldn't stop the incessant tap of her foot against the pavement nor the continuous tugging of her hair. And that sick churning feeling in her belly warned she may well have made a fool of herself the previous evening. Maybe she'd been too eager – too easy to please? *What if I came off as desperate!*

That's what living without a partner for fourteen years did to you – eroded your confidence, turned your thoughts inward, and put you out of practice with the dating game. It didn't help that the first streaks of silver were threading through her hair, and at forty-one years old, she'd well and truly lost the bloom of youth.

Heat scalded her face as she sensed the not-so-covert ogles and craning necks of Bindarra Creek's notorious gaggle of busy-bodies. They sat about two metres behind her bundled up in coats and jackets, at the table closest to the open door that led inside the Cyprus Café. Natalie had firsthand knowledge that these old ladies were fundamentally kind to their souls. However, their immense kindness was matched by their equally unwavering desire to meddle in other people's lives.

Puffing out a slow breath that she hoped would steady her racing heart, she willed her hand away from her hair and picked up her mobile to check the time. Yet again. Ten-fifteen a.m. He'd definitely said eight o'clock when they'd parted ways last night outside the Riverside Pub's bistro after having dinner together. It had taken every scrap of confidence she possessed to attend that meeting, and every scrap of courage to put herself out there in the app dating world in the first place. But she was tired of having no one to share the highs and lows of everyday life. Tired of having no one to laugh and cry with. Although she loved him with every fibre of her being, her sixteen-year-old son didn't quite fill the void left by her dead husband. Besides, it wouldn't be long before Noah would be off – living his own life and even though she'd made friends during the three years she'd lived in the small town, it wasn't the same as having a loving partner by her side. Once Noah was out experiencing the world, she would truly be alone. Most of all she missed the companionship – all of which had led her to linger at the café for the man she'd been matched with, to turn up.

She dropped her mobile onto the red-checked table-cloth and looked around for the waitress, but she'd disappeared inside the warmer café – no doubt to avoid the chill. She'd be inside herself if there had been any vacant tables. This morning, the yoga class had run over time. When she'd arrived, the café had been crammed full of pensioners and a few intrepid joggers.

Another blast of wind frosted her cold face. No way

would she wait for her erstwhile date any longer. A tiny flicker of annoyance burst into life, dominating her previous thoughts of inadequacy and smothering her normally cautious nature. She was worth more than being stood up. She'd track down the wanker and tell him to his face how disrespectful was his behaviour. Fuelled by her rising indignation, she dug her credit card out of her shoulder-bag and waved it in the air.

"Are you waiting for someone?" Bracelets jangled as a wrinkled hand pulled out the vacant chair next to her, and an elderly lady with braided grey hair almost reaching her waist, plopped into the seat. Ms Edwina Lette. The leader of the gang. She dropped her scarlet yoga mat beside feet clad in a pair of muddy pink gumboots and brushed her fringe away from needle-sharp eyes. The puffer-jacket she wore made her scrawny frame appear plumper than normal.

Too late. Natalie should have bolted when she'd had the chance. The remaining two chairs grated as they also were dragged out when two other elderly women claimed them. Florrie Miller, the newly ordained Church of England vicar and Pamela Brown – both as lethal as Ms Lette but in very different ways. A quick glance over her shoulder revealed the less dangerous member of the nosey mob, Mrs Beatrix Fukuka, was deep in conversation with Therese Morgan, whose white hair shone like a holy beacon when a shot of sunlight broke through the heavy clouds.

Pamela Brown picked up one of Natalie's empty mugs and frowned as she peered inside at the dregs. She tutted, her back ramrod straight. "All that coffee on an empty stomach is no good for you. Have the Greek scrambled eggs and avocado toast. I'll wave Thea over so you can order."

"There's no need... I was just leaving... " Her face hotter

than a furnace, Natalie attempted to deflect their attention. She shouldn't have bothered.

Edwina interrupted. "Now, if you'd had a pot of tea, I could have read your tea leaves and told you when a handsome man will appear in your life. Or – perhaps he already has?" She winked as she leaned forward in a conspiratorial manner. "Tessa had dinner at the Riverside Pub last night with that lovely doctor, Emma Fahey. She told me all about how she saw you there with your new beau. A distinguished-looking fellow with silver hair, I believe. *And* he's our new guest at Fig Tree Lodge. Our only guest, if I'm honest but not a bad catch. I caught a glimpse of him yesterday morning when he arrived. Very tasty." She smacked her lips with gusto.

Natalie cringed. *Kill me now.*

A group of teenagers dawdled into view, laughing and jostling each other, school backpacks slung over shoulders hunched against the biting winter wind. One kid even dragged his bag along the ground with little thought to the damage being caused.

Natalie spied the familiar, tousled dark-brown hair of her only child. "Noah!" Her screech reeked of *'save me!'*.

Noah flung a startled glance toward her, his eyes widening as he took in the women flanking her on both sides. Ducking his head, he gave a half-hearted wave and slunk behind Drew Taylor, whose bright red hair was covered by a woolly beanie knitted in Bindarra Creek's high school colours. Natalie recognised it as one of the beanies his adoptive mother Abby had made a few months ago when she'd attended a Country Women's Association's craft session. "Sorry, Mum. Can't stop. We're late for class."

The group sent hunted looks towards the occupants of

the table before picking up their lagging pace until they all but sprinted down the footpath.

Late! At after ten o'clock they were more than late, and Natalie made a mental note to question Noah when he got home from school. She gazed longingly at his rapidly retreating form, before girding her loins and turning to face her interrogators. "Morning again, ladies. I really enjoyed Tessa's yoga class this morning. What did you think of the new routine?"

With the unwavering determination of a killer shark circling its prey, Edwina ignored Natalie's feeble diversion tactic. "I do like a man who knows how to dress, and dimples in chins have always made me weak at the knees." She emitted a dramatic sigh and fanned her face. "A couple of years ago there was this Pom I had the hots for. A little younger than me but I always fancied myself as a bit of a cougar…"

Pamela interrupted her oldest friend with a rude snort. "Nobody is interested in your fantasies, Edwina. Besides, at your age it's ridiculous the way you carry on."

"I'll have you know they are not fantasies."

"That's made me think of a theme for this week's sermon." Seemingly oblivious to her friends' snappy exchange, Florrie Miller rested her elbow on the table and cupped her chin. Her short, greying brown hair poked out from her woolly Sea Eagles beanie like tufts of straw. "Trust - how social media has impacted on our ability to trust others."

"Trust has nothing to do with it." Edwina jabbed Natalie in the ribs with a bony finger. "It's all about the sex. Nothing reduces stress levels like sex. In saying that, I'm not so sure about this new man of yours, Natalie. Only this morning as I was looking for my push-up bra, I had a premonition." She sank back in her chair and folded her arms, her narrow gaze pinning Natalie in place like a nail gun.

"A premonition? That's a new one. I'm surprised your dear-departed aunt Matilda wasn't whispering in your ear." Pamela Brown gave a haughty sniff, her narrow face settling into disapproving lines.

Edwina scowled. "Actually, it's been a while since Matilda's been around. She must be busy."

"What rubbish. This insistence on communicating with ghosts has to stop." Pamela rolled her eyes.

"I'm serious. But I must admit I'm getting worried."

"About your ghost?" Natalie could feel her mouth drop at the idea.

"Absolutely. She has never been absent for this long in all the years I've lived in Fig Tree Lodge. Basically, that's most of my life."

Natalie shivered as another gust of wind scattered wet leaves down the footpath and swept over her bare arms. Her thick parka would have been a better choice than the short-sleeved tunic dress she'd pulled on after changing from her yoga gear. She'd hoped the emerald colour would heighten the green flecks in her hazel eyes. A pointless effort considering the man she'd intended to impress had failed to appear.

Buy links: https://books2read.com/u/4ElrYg

A Bindarra Creek Mystery Romance – released from July 2022
Amulet of Death – Suzanne Gilchrist (aka S E Gilchrist)
Beyond the Gate – Rhonda Forrest

Protecting their Destiny – Erin Moira O'Hara
Only She Knew – Linda Charles
Secrets of River Cottage – Annie Seaton
Forgotten Secrets – Susanne Bellamy
A Perfect Danger – Phillipa Nefri Clark

About the Bindarra Creek Series

Welcome to Bindarra Creek, a struggling country town where people work hard and love deeply. Set in the picturesque tablelands of New England, Australia, Bindarra Creek is a fictional, rural community full of romance, intrigue, adventure, drama and suspense.

To date there are four multi-author 'series' set in the Bindarra Creek world all written by best-selling Australian romance authors. A fifth is planned for late 2022 – **A Bindarra Creek Christmas.**

Bindarra Creek A Town Reborn

Take Me Home – Suzanne Gilchrist (aka S E Gilchrist)
In the Heat of the Night – Susanne Bellamy
No Looking Back - Linda Charles
Worth the Wait – Annie Seaton
With Every Breath – Lauren K. McKellar
Stealing Her Heart – Simone Angela
A Twist of Fate – Erin Moira O'Hara
Promise Me Forever – Juanita Kees

Bindarra Creek Short & Sweet

What's in a Kiss – Linda Charles
My Forever Valentine – Sandie James (not available)
Pearls and Green Beer – Susanne Bellamy
Full Circle – Annie Seaton
Date with Destiny – Erin Moira O'Hara
A Letter From the Queen – Lee Christine
Love's Sweet Challenge – Suzanne Gilchrist (aka S E Gilchrist)
The Widow Maker – Lauren K. McKellar
Out of the Blue – Noelle Clark

Bindarra Creek Romance

Bindarra Creek Makeover - S. E. Gilchrist
Shadows of the Heart - Lee Christine
Second Chance Love - Susanne Bellamy
The CEO Mechanic - Sandie James (not available)
Reach for the Stars - Kerrie Paterson
Home to Bindarra Creek - Juanita Kees
Stolen Sanctuary - Stacey Nash
Tempting Fate - Erin Moira O'Hara
One More Day - Linda Charles
The Vine - Lauren K. McKellar
The Ghost of His Past - Simone Angela
Joanie's Dilemma - Marianne Theresa
Buckley's Chance - Noelle Clark

Full details on buy links for all books in Bindarra Creek
world can be found at:
www.bindarracreekromance.com

By Phillipa Nefri Clark

Rivers End Mystery Romances

The Stationmaster's Cottage

Jasmine Sea

The Secrets of Palmerston House

The Christmas Key

Taming the Wind

Martha

Daphne Jones Mysteries

Daph on the Beach (prequel)

Till Daph Do Us Part

The Shadow of Daph

Tales of Life and Daph

Bindarra Creek Rural Fiction

A Perfect Danger

Tangled by Tinsel

Maple Gardens Matchmakers

The Heart Match

The Christmas Match

Doctor Grok's Peculiar Shop Short Story Collection

Last Known Contact

(A gripping standalone crime/romantic suspense)

Simple Words for Troubled Times

(Short non-fiction happiness and comfort book)

Prefer Audiobooks?

The Stationmaster's Cottage

Jasmine Sea

The Secrets of Palmerston House

Last Known Contact

Simple Words for Troubled Times

Till Daph Do Us Part

About the Author

Phillipa lives just outside a beautiful town in country Victoria, Australia. She also lives in the many worlds of her imagination and stockpiles stories beside her laptop.

She writes from the heart about love, dreams, secrets, discovery, the sea, the world as she knows it... or wishes it could be. She loves happy endings, heart-pounding suspense, and characters who stay with you long after the final page.

With a passion for music, the ocean, animals, nature, reading, and writing, she is often found in the vegetable garden pondering a new story.

Phillipa's Website

A Perfect Danger

Copyright © 2023 Phillipa Nefri Clark

Cover design by Annie Seaton
Editing by Nas Dean